WEST WINDS' FOOL

and Other Stories of the Devil's West

LAURA ANNE GILMAN

Book View Café

Cover Art: Rebecca Flaum (Studio Catawampus)
Cover Design: Natania Barron
Editor: Leah Cutter
Project Manager: Patricia Burroughs for BookViewCafe.com
Production Manager: April Steenburgh

ISBN: 978-1-61138-772-8

Contents

For April. For infinite reasons.

Introduction

The Territory was never planned. None of this was planned, not really.

In 2010, I was writer-in-residence at the Odyssey Workshop in New Hampshire. During one session I asked my students to write an introductory paragraph with an antagonist, a protagonist, and a narrator. And, because I'm cruel but fair, I did the exercise along with them.

It was meant to be a throwaway, a jump-off point for that day's discussion. But the opening line of that paragraph—*"The rider came to the crossroads just shy of noon, where a man dressed all in black stared up at another man hanging from a gallows"*—lingered long after the class, long after the session. And, eventually, it became the opening line to the story "Crossroads."

And the Territory—although I didn't know it at the time—was born. Just a nugget, a kernel of an idea, that the lands to the west of the Mississippi and east of Spanish California, contained a magic, and a danger, beyond what history books told us.

"Crossroads" sold to Fantasy Magazine, and got a

positive reaction, enough that editor John Joseph Adams asked me to write another "weird west" story for him. And so, "The Devil's Jack" came into being, and was published in the anthology *Dead Man's Hand*. And I stared at the two stories, and realized that there was a lot more there than I'd been aware of. A *lot* more.

Sometimes, the writer is the last to figure shit out.

So I sat down to write another story in the universe. Something with a female protagonist this time, I thought. A young woman, maybe, to counter the more jaded characters we'd already seen. And maybe this time, we'd actually *see* the Devil who'd only been mentioned in the previous stories.

But about 10,000 words into the then-titled "A Town Called Flood," I realized that this ... was not going to be a short story. Or even a novella. And so I called up my then-agent and said, "I think ... I have my next book idea."

And from that—eventually—came *Silver On The Road*. And an entire bookcase of research materials, a wall of marked-up maps, and a handful of notebooks filled with ideas, characters, historical detours, and what-ifs.

And now, eight years, three award nominations, and nearly 500,000 words later, I'm still on the Road, still finding pockets and characters within the Territory with stories to tell. I may be here for the rest of my life.

I can think of far worse places to live.

I hope you'll enjoy the ride with me.

Crossroads

John came to the crossroads at just shy of noon, where a man dressed all in black was staring up at another man hanging from a gallowstree. No, not hanging; he was being hung, the loop still slack around his neck, his body dangling mid-air. That, John thought, his pack heavy on his shoulder and his hat pulled low, was not something a wise man would get involved in. And yet, he could not resist asking, "What did he do?"

The man in black turned around and glared at John. "He asked too many impertinent questions."

The man with the rope around his neck laughed at that, a rueful, amused sound, and John decided he liked the dead man.

"You might want to move on," the man in black continued in a voice that wasn't a suggestion. "This is a bad place to be for a lone traveler."

"Looks like he might agree," John said, but slung his pack off his shoulder, resting it on the ground, and looked up at the hanging man. "You okay with this?"

"It's not my first choice for nuncheon," the man admitted, but did not try to explain or ask for help.

John stepped forward and around, circling the man in black and coming up alongside the gallowstree, carefully out of reach of the hanging man's potential to kick. They were both long, lean men, their boots spit-shone where John's were dusty and worn. The man in black was staring at the hanging man, who seemed to be watching something far over the horizon, unconcerned by his predicament.

John studied them both. Crossroads were bad places. Magicians and devils were bad news. Dusk and dawn and noon overhead were bad times. Every child knew that. This wasn't his place, this wasn't his business. It wasn't his responsibility. He should just move on, and not get involved. Let them do what they would do, and be done.

A prickling against his chest reminded him it wasn't all that simple, for him. His hand touched the side of the pack, feeling the smooth leather, the shape of his belongings below. He breathed in through his nose, out through his mouth. The air was warm already, and filled with the dust of the road.

Sunrise and sunset, and high noon overhead. The crossroads. Places and times of transit, of coming upon and slipping away. Power ebbed and flowed and could be taken from another, if you knew how.

John knew what he was about, as another might not. He had sworn an oath.

Every step of the road was a choice.

"Some things, there's no real choice at all," he said softly, and slid his hand under the flap of the pack, his fingers touching cool metal.

"Stay out of this, boy," the man in black said, misinterpreting his action.

John hadn't been a boy in decades. The slip made the edge of his mouth curl slightly, even as he tilted his head to look at the man in the black from under the brim of his hat. Magician or devil, it made no difference to John. Immortals were always trouble. Two immortals meant twice as much trouble.

The silver flask under his fingers seemed to almost shiver, and John drew it out slowly, not allowing his actions to be misinterpreted. "Was just planning to drink your health," he said to the hanging man, raising the flask in salute. "Might I know your name afore you aren't using it no more?"

"Benjamin," the hanging man said. "Benjamin West."

Magician, then. Magicians took their names from one

of the four weatherly winds. Devils took their names from their masters.

"Your memory, master Benjamin West," John said, and took a swig. Cool, fresh water washed down his throat. Others might think he carried rotgut or whiskey; water was safer. Water couldn't be magicked. Silver and water, and the dead man's name; that should cover all possibilities.

"So what question did he ask?"

The man in black had turned back to the hanging man, his hands raised as though to cast the final spell. John's question arrested the movement, although the man's back and shoulders did not betray any emotion.

"Why do you care?"

John shrugged, letting the silver flask hang from his hand, casually. "Naturally curious?"

"I wanted to know where he got that lovely walking stick." The hanging man's voice was filled with laughter. Laughing at himself, laughing at John.

John didn't look around for a stick, but kept his gaze on the man in black. He wasn't so easily caught, him: the dead man was as dangerous as the man in black, and only a fool lost sight of that. "Is that so?"

"What do you think?" The man in black's voice was gritty and hard now, and although he lowered his arms, he didn't turn around.

"Must have been hell of a question you didn't want to answer." John took another swig from the flask, his body loose and gangly, just passin' time, three strangers on the road. A tip of the flask, here, and a step and a step and a third step away, then another tip of the flask. Bare splutters in the dust, a dark splatter left behind. Step and a step and a step, all the way around the gallowstree, all the way around the man in black and the hanging man: locking all three within. Locking any innocents out.

"If you're to kill him, don't let my bein' here pause you," John said conversationally as he walked, taking another sip when he was done. "I've no mule in this pull."

A hesitation in the breath of the world. John's fingers sweated against the cool silver, his pack abandoned outside the circle, the leather shape casting a low shadow on the dirt. The dead man's gaze sharpened like he saw something coming over that horizon, and the man in black growled. John felt the sharp knife of risk scratch against his spine, but merely let his fingers rest on the flask, and studied the sun overhead.

"Mighty warm out, once sun hits directly. Be a mercy to finish him off by then. Or not, ifn' that's what you're aiming for."

The flask was near-empty now, and it shimmered again under his hand, like a warning. The man in black had no choice but to choose, and now. John felt the first whisper of enchantment like the roll of thunder in the distance, barely recognizable until it swept down over the plains and knocked you out of the saddle or off your feet. The dead man didn't move, not resigned so much as simply waiting. They had forgotten John now, dismissed him in the greater business of their battle.

Ignored, he tilted the silver flask in the four directions, making an offering of spirit if not flesh, and then tilted it in towards the center of his water-bound circle, to where the two magicians posed, gathering their will.

The wind was still, the air silent, the sun too hot for a spring afternoon. A normal man, a man set about his own business, would think it odd; suspect a storm rising, or a predator in the woods. John let his breath exhale, and waited.

The sun shifted, barely a twitch in the shadows, and the man in black set himself hard against the ground and raised his arms until they mirrored the sun, settling into position directly above.

"Hang or fly," the hanging man said, lifting his hands to the midpoint of his chest, palms pressed together, fingers likewise pointing toward the sky.

Magician duels were iffy things. To chance upon one was rare and risky, and it could easily all go wrong. John moved his arm slow, taking that last drink of water. Silver and fresh water, and a dead man's name.

The man in black did not move but his shadow did, the first direct shaft of sunlight dancing it forward, reaching up and yanking the rope tight. The hanging man jerked, legs kicking high and arms falling low, and the shadow swarmed but John moved faster, the water in his mouth spitting high and clear.

Shadow and water met, spluttering and sparking like an old campfire, and the man in black swore but did not turn. A battle of nerves now, as the hanging man danced and stilled, water dripping down shadow, shadow sizzling-dry water, and the dead man's power hanging between them.

John had no sweat, no moisture for his breath, everything he had gone to tie him into the battle raging around him. The silver flask fell to the ground and water spilled into the dirt, his throat cracking and swelling like the fever had taken him, but he did not relent.

Magicians named themselves for one of the four winds, drifting across the surface of the earth, unstoppable, mostly unseen. And they killed each other; only each other, never anyone else, and so nobody cared, because one less magician in the world did nobody harm. But John knew better. One magician dead meant one less magician, not one less bit of magic.

Killer had claim, killer took the power, and made it his own. Master Benjamin West had been caught and killed fair by his rules; but their rules didn't allow for someone like John.

Clean water and pure silver, and the strength of his oath to drive him.

The man in black whispered one single word, sweet and ragged, too strange for John to hear but it hit the air like a rock into water. The rope turned bronze, then black under the direct noon light, and the hanging man's skin seemed to ripple, like wheat under wind, and tightened around his bones.

"Give over," the man in black ordered. "Fair caught, fair bound, under the midday sun. Give over. It is mine."

"Take it," the dead man said, but meant "if you can."

Thunder cracked. The air smelt burnt, the dry dust at their feet swirling faintly. Magic filled the air with a deep, ugly black-blue John felt his skin crawl, sweat now running under his clothing like a summer's blast, but he held steady, bending to pick up the silver flask. He held it with its mouth angled out and up toward the two, as though offering them a drink, though neither paid him any heed. The water he had dripped into the soil sizzled, and the magic curled back around, turning like eddies in a stream.

"I will take it," the man in black said, and clenched his fingers together. The dead man's skin burst into flames, the rope squeezing tight, and his heels kicked up, drumming at the air. The man in black sucked in his breath, and the magic streamed toward him.

Magic went to the strongest, the quickest, the most

determined to win. But that did not mean it always went to the magician.

"Benjamin West," John whispered. The flask shimmered, filling; clear water resisting the magic's pull, holding it still and safe. A dead man's name bound the magic he once held while breath still warmed his lungs, if not one beat longer.

The man in black, cheated, snarled, and the dead man danced at the end of his rope, and John screwed the cap on tight.

The man in black turned, clenching his hands in anger, even as afternoon light filled the spaces and painted the hanging man's shadow with long strokes on the ground behind him.

"You cannot use it," the man in black said, his voice gritty and soft, the voice of a man who already knows more than he can exploit, and yet always wants more. "You have not the skill."

"It went to the man quick enough to catch it," John replied, feeling the menace in the man's voice, even as he slipped a hand under his coat, and let the silver star pinned beneath shine. "Usin' it's not my intention."

They stared at each other, deadly calm, and then John turned, stepping across the circle to where his pack waited. Silver and pure water, and sigil-cut rounds for his gun hung low and ready at his hip. A wise man was prepared. A smart man was ready. A lawman in these territories needed to be both, and more.

He slid the flask back under the flap, closing the lacing tight. "What's done is done, and done square and fair." It was not a threat, merely an observation of fact. When he turned around again, the man in black was gone.

John tilted his head back, the brim of his hat still shading his eyes. The sun would be past-direct in a matter of moments. The crossroads was now safe for travelers; he could move on.

"A good day, sirs," he said to the afternoon air, for it never harmed a man to be polite, and walked out of the crossroads, the hanging man slack and sunlit behind him.

The Devil's Jack

T he horse was an old one, and piebald to boot, warning he'd go lame sooner rather than not, but Jack would be damned if he'd give up and walk.

T he fact that his stubbornness came too late for his soul didn't make him any more willing to relent.

"Whoa now, hoss," he said, sawing back gently on the reins held in his left hand, shifting his weight to ease the ache in his buttocks, and squinting at the horizon. The smudge in the distance might be an outcropping of stone… or it might be yet another hallucination brought on by exhaustion and hope.

Only way to find out was to ride on.

The sun had shifted to the western half of the sky, casting his shadow odd-angled in front of them, a beast with four legs and two heads and a sway to its movement that looked more like a shambles-beast than anything living.

There were days Jack wondered himself, if they'd already died and been too stubborn to fall.

But if he'd have died, the devil would have called his name for sure.

"We're still here, hoss," he told the piebald. "For all the good it does us."

The horse had no opinion. It lifted one foot in front of the other with weary determination, moving forward across the broken plain because going back was not an option, and they neither of them were fool enough to stop.

Hooves hitting stone woke Jack from his riding doze, the change from the softer clodding of dirt and dust jarring his senses into full alertness as much as the singing of an arrow or the smell of black powder.

He'd been right: rock, an entire massive ridge cresting out of the hill, solid and deep. Deep enough down to touch the core of the world. Deep enough down to be protection, for a little while. Jack let out a sigh and the piebald's sides heaved in echo, its head drooping down to its knees.

"Yeah, you're a good hoss," he said, patting the withers with almost-affection. "Time for a rest."

Swinging out of the saddle, his thighs protested the move, and his feet ached with the weight of his body, but the press of his boot-soles against rock was a sweet pain.

He paused, almost unwilling to breathe, but the rock remained steady underfoot, and his thoughts stayed his own.

Deep enough, for a while.

Unhooking the canteen from his saddle, Jack took a long swig, wiped his mouth with the back of his hand and considered pouring the rest over his head, to wash the dust and grime from his skin.

"No, hoss. Can't do that," he said. "No telling who how long we might be here."

Not that long, never that long; soon enough he would have to move on, driven to another town, or farmstead, or fugitive's trail.

Slipping the reins over the horse's head, he looped them loosely through the stirrup so they wouldn't drag, and stepped forward, trusting the piebald to follow behind.

The ridge was lumped like the bare bones of a

skeleton, dusty-dry and rust red. Not even moss grew on them, here under the blazing sun.

Hard rock was good. Hard rock was safe.

For now, experience told him. Don't you dare relax.

There were strips of jerky in his saddlebag, and another canteen of water, half-full and stale, but drinkable. The piebald could graze and drink when they came to pastures, but Jack had not sat to a meal without worry since longer than he could easy remember.

"No," he said, thinking back. "Two weeks past? The riverboat, coming up past Louistown."

Water was safe, too. Water and stone.

Stone was better, though. The devil couldn't reach through that much stone.

"Y ou played. You lost."

The gambler had a jovial look that Jack had distrusted at once. But only a fool trusted the man who held the deck, and Jack had prided himself on being no fool. Young, yes, and green, he owned to that, but never foolish. He sat warily and played carefully and never bet more than he could afford to lose. That was how you got to be old, in the Devil's West.

"I played and I lost and you've taken your winnings," Jack said. "And now I'll be stepping away from the table, like a sober man."

More sober now than he'd been an hour before: the dealer had a run of luck that could only be cursed, and every card that turned called out for mortals to beware, until the river turned and drowned him, once and for all.

And the other men at the table had breathed a sigh of relief, that it had been Jack, and not them.

"Leaving, broke and sober. Tis often the fate of mortal man," the dealer agreed, and his jovial expression was only kind. Jack's left hand flexed, feeling for the gun that did not hang by his side.

You removed your weapons before you sat at the table. The saloon girl with the saucy eye held it for him, his gun and his hat, and no way to reach either before he was dead. The fact that every soul in the saloon was in the same boat did not warm Jack, not with the way the dealer watched his face, and not his hands. This dealer feared no powder and shot, nor an arrow from ambush, or a knife in the dark.

Jack had known who he played with, when he slid his coin across the felt. That had been the point. That was why men came here, to test their luck. He swallowed, the sick feeling he had at the loss—everything he had, from cash to horse—eclipsed by a worse sensation in his gut. Not two years on his own, and he had failed, utterly. The devil cherished the prideful, his mentor had warned him, the better to break them of it.

"One more hand, to win it all," the dealer said, and his hands moved over the cards, shuffling them without sound. "One more hand to win it all, and more."

It was a devil's bargain, in the heart of the devil's town, and only a green-sapped fool would have taken it.

But Jack-as-was had not been as wise as he thought.

The rock eased his pain, and Jack slept soundly on its hard embrace, no darkly sounding whisper searching for him, poisoning his rest. That knowledge had been hard-won and cherished, that through the solid rock and shifting water, the bones and blood of the earth, the devil could not call.

Before the sun rose, he woke, curled under a rough blanket, still fully dressed save his boots, those tied to the piebald's saddle to keep scorpions or worse from making them a home.

He had played that final hand: and lost. The fruit of his bargain, the payment of his debt: Seven years and seven and seven again, he was bound. The devil's dog, the devil's errand-boy. But there was a loophole: if he did not hear the call, he could not be summoned. If he could not be summoned, he could not do the devil's work.

It must amuse his master to play this game, to let Jack play at it, the days and weeks he could avoid the call, only to yank him back the moment he came within reach. Seven years and seven and seven again to pay, and nearly sixteen of them gone now, along with even the memory of the things he had hoped to regain. Sixteen was eight twice: numbers of protection, for normal men, but there was no protection for Jack, save water and stone, and that lasted only so long. If he died while bound, he was the devil's forevermore.

Jack had long ago lost the taste for living, but he had no intention of dying any time soon. He rose, and stretched, saluting the morning sun stretching clear across the face of the outcrop, the sky still clouded and dim behind him.

"Human."

Jack turned and spun, reaching not for the pistol that once pressed against his thigh but the packet of herbs he now carried in the holster, the dried bits catching in the wind as he scattered them, a free-moving arc of glittering brown-green.

"That's hardly polite," another voice said, this time

behind him, and it sounded both amused and hurt. Two? More? Or one demon, inhumanly fast?

Magicians roamed these lands, and demons, and the devil. Jack feared none of them, any more, but lack of fear did not mean lack of caution.

"You came to us, and slept in our home. We came merely to say good morn, and you react…thus?"

Two… no, four, or five, from the shadows that crept around him. Slender and dark-skinned like savages, bare in their skins, dark hair long and wild, braided with feathers of impossibly bright colors, like a fancy-girl's beads. Like humans, until you saw them move, joints turning too smoothly, eyes glittering too bright. Until you saw the shimmer like heatstroke, under their skin.

The herbs had pushed them back, but they had not fled.

The horse, dumb beast that it was, shifted its weight from leg to leg, but did not otherwise react. It had seen far worse, in its time under Jack's leg.

"We don't scare you?"

"Only a damned man isn't cautious around demon," Jack replied. He couldn't tell which one spoke, they moved so restlessly, and he didn't want to watch their mouths, not so close to those glittering eyes. "Never heard of your kind taking to hard rock, before." It wasn't a question—even a damned man did not ask a demon questions it might answer.

"You know many demon, then, human. To carry bane, and not a pistol, to wear the sigil instead of a cross?"

He'd never worn a cross, not even back then. The sigil on a thong around his neck wasn't much more use—but it showed a certain amount of respect.

Demons and magicians knew the Hanging Man, who had been here long before the bleeding god.

"I'm the devil's Jack," he said, having no desire to play their game. "You may have heard of me."

They hissed, but did not back away. The devil had no claim on them, as soulless as the piebald. But they would—most like—not interfere with his dog, either.

"We grant you the use of our rock," one of them said. "You may remain as long as you like." Mocking: they knew he could not remain, dared not stay too long.

"I may leave freely, then." Again, not a question, but merely to confirm: to make them agree, and not slide a card out from their sleeve.

"Yes. Yes, blasted human, you may."

They could not. Their words, the tone of their words, gave them away. They had been bound to this hard ridge—some magician exercising his power, for some reason only magicians understood.

A wise man and a damned man both avoided thinking too much why a magician did anything.

"You could stay, and amuse us," another one said. "We are so terribly bored."

That was why they had come to him, then. Something new on this barren ridge, to distract them. He felt no pity: they were demon. And yet, to be trapped on this ridge, for however long, was not a fate he would wish on any creature.

He had spoken truth, earlier: demon did not take to hard stone. They lingered on river banks and in shadowed caves, not here under the hot dry sun. "No doubt some terrible act angered a magician that he bound you here, with no release."

"Not so terrible. Not so anger-making. He was far more terrible than we, and woe to the human who bore him. His magic would have ripped him from her womb, and burnt her to ashes from the hot malice in his bones."

Magicians were made, not born. Self-made, given to the madness of the winds. But there was something in the demon's tone that made the story ring true.

Not that Jack would ever know, one way or another. Yet, demon had no reason to lie for sheer meanness; they were no more evil than a tornado, merely set on having their way no matter what another might wish or do.

Much like humans, he knew. It was a rare soul who came at you with unselfish good. It simply wasn't the way the world had been made.

This ridge offered a night of safety, but a lack of evil did not mean a lack of harm, from tornado or demon, and a wise man got out of the way of both.

"I'll water and feed my hoss, and be gone," he said. "No need to fret yourselves on my account."

They stared at him like wolves in winter stare at elk, and he lowered his head and set his shoulders, same as the elk might do. Do not mess with me, his posture warned. You might win, but you would not like the cost.

They stared, and then scattered, gone as swift as they'd come, and the piebald and he were alone on the rocky ridge.

The ridge ran some distance toward the north, and Jack walked it through the morning, not pausing when the sun reached devil's peak and bore down on him, rivulets of grimy sweat sticking his shirt and pants' legs to his skin. The piebald's girth was loose, its step slow and steady, and every now and again it reached over to nip at Jack's hair in a gesture of what he thought might well be affection. Or hunger.

"Grazing for you, soon enough," he promised it. "Just a bit longer more." The ability to stretch his legs without worry was sweeter than fresh water. He would have to leave this haven soonish, and be on his way, but not just yet.

He thought, safe on rock, of his mother, and his sister. His teachers, back East. His first riding companion, near twenty years back, who had taken the green youth, new-come to the Territory, under his arm and taught him how to survive.

Old Matthew, who'd died north of Smithtown when the savages overran their camp. Died by his own hand, rather than be taken captive. "Never let them take you," Mattie had said. "Never do anything other than by your own free will. Promise yourself now, to never give up that will."

He had been, in the end, no better a student to Matty than he had been at hauling a plow.

Those memories were only safe on rock, and they never did him any good. Jack forced his mind to considering each step, the colors and striations of the rock, the crunch of his boot heel on timeworn rubble, and the sough of the wind against his ears, until his brain went numb once more.

Finally, the day came to a close, and while the ridge ran on a while more, there was the blur of blue shadow in the distance that told Jack there was a town off to the south.

People—settlers and traders, common folk—were wary of him, knowing without being told there was something gone wrong with him, but he missed hearing them speak, even when they did not speak to him. To sit, briefly, at a table, and pretend he could stay... it broke him, every time, and yet still he could not resist.

If he was fortunate, his master would have no summons for him.

B riar, the sign at the boundary-line named the town, and it seemed well-called: sparse and spare, the color of deadwood and sand. But the buildings were sturdy, and the children clean and strong-limbed, and the sound of their play was the first thing he heard, when he rode into town. They were isolated enough, out here, they need fear nothing come up on them without warning from the lookout perched above the church spire.

"Trust in God but Watch the Border" was inscribed at the archway of that church, and Jack stared at it a while before riding on. Churches were rare here, where the devil held sway. The saloon looked clean and orderly, and Jack barely hesitated before swinging down off the piebald's back, wincing as his soles touched dirt.

Silence. Silence in his head, silence in his bones.

Looping the piebald's reins around the post, he gave it a pat and a cube of close-hoarded sugar, and went through the sand-brown doors of the Briar's Last Hope.

A s usual, the folk gave him a wary circle: other strangers might be pestered for news, or begged for a story, but they left him to his table and his whiskey, the girl serving him a plate of something that looked well-marbled but tasted of gristle and bone. He ate it, and the dry potatoes, and drank his whiskey, and let the noise wash over him, better than any bath he'd ever had.

And then it came.

No words: there were never words, only the command. The game was over, for the nonce: He had all-unwitting come where his master wanted him, were men waited, dreading, unknowing, for his hand on their necks.

Ten men of Briar, sold of their own free will to the devil, waiting only to be claimed.

"All right," he said, as though he had a choice. His meal done, he would rise up—no more avoiding the dirt that clung to him, now that the deed was done—and walk through the town, and find who had taken his master's coin.

Whatever border they sought to guard, whatever god they trusted, it had not been enough.

They were waiting for him when he came: nine of them, gathered on the church steps.

"Avram ran," the oldest of them said, when Jack put one foot on the faded wooden steps, and looked up at them, his hat angled back so they could see most of his face in the light coming from the open door behind them. "He broke and ran when we knew you were coming."

Word had spread: like the demon, the townsfolk of Briar had heard of the devil's Jack. "But you waited."

"We did what we had to do. Our children are safe. That is all that matters."

Their calm was almost disturbing. The damned bargained. The damned wept. The damned offered you everything they no longer possessed. They did not stand like god-fearing men.

"The border. On your sign. What is it?" You could ask humans questions you did not of demons. They would lie just as easily—but they did not always, and there was no risk in listening.

They looked at each other, the nine men of Briar, and if they wondered at his question, they did not show it. Finally one, neither oldest nor youngest, spoke. "A magician lived here, back before there was a town. Bitter and sour, and not able to stop fiddling with things that would not be under his control. And in his fiddling, in his disregard for what was natural, he called up the briar-rock from the breast of the earth, and let loose abominations on the land. The founders of this town contained it, somehow. Built a border around the town. But they left no instructions, no grimoire we could follow, when the ground rumbled underfoot last year, and the first abomination returned."

It had the sound of a story long-told, worn with the repetition. And cleansing silver would do no good against demon, not so many, not when they held a grudge. "You've no magicians, none to hire or lure, to strengthen the barrier? " Better to bargain with a magician and risk his whim, than sell your soul outright.

Another man, a freeman from his skin, as upright as the others, spoke then: "There was no time. The devil was there."

"Yes. He often is." Jack's words were dry, but the townsmen took them as solemn gospel.

"And now you will take us." The freeman again, resigned.

He was the devil's dog, sent to retrieve what was owe. "Yes."

"Does it hurt?"

He could not tell who had asked that question, a voice within the group. "Yes." Now, and forever. That was what it meant, to give over to the devil. Not a great pain, not always, but a never-ending one. The sour bile of regrets; the loss of hope; the abandonment of fleeting, innocent joy for the more grim knowledge of sorrow. He felt them all, scraping at his insides.

They would exist within that pain, their soul's protection forfeit, for the rest of eternity. For protecting their home.

Sixteen years of taking the devil's price had hardened Jack to regret. But these were good men. Honest men, who had waited for their fate. Looking at them, something inside Jack rebelled.

"Go make your peace with your families," he said. "No memories will save you now, but there is no reason to leave them with pain."

Lie to them, he meant. Give them a pretty story to believe. They won't, but they will remember that you tried.

"I'll be back come dawn. Don't make me have to find you."

He had some hard riding to do, before then.

The moon rose low and cold in the sky, and the devil pinpricked him the whole ride back to the rock ridge, but Jack gritted his teeth and clenched his jaw and did not relent, even when the pricks became jabs, and the jabs drew blood from his skin.

The devil was always there, but he could not be everywhere. So long as he did not turn his full attention here, Jack had a chance.

No. Jack had no chance. He let the thought go, became empty and bare as the grasslands around him, all life hiding away the closer he came to the demons' rock.

They met him on the lowest ridge, five sleek shadows glowing and shifting under the moonlight. This was their time, their place, and he was no longer a stranger to them, that they would hide their true form.

He had never thought to gamble, again. Never thought to bargain, or hide a card in his sleeve. Had thought he had nothing left to place in the pot.

He stopped, the horse's hooves barely settled on the rocky spine, and called to them. "What would you risk, to be entertained?"

"What would we not, to no longer be bored," came back the answer. "Have you come to be our fool, human?"

"I am already my own fool," he said. "But if you can manage it, you will have entertainment—and strike a blow against the memory of the magician who bound you here."

That had their attention, he could tell by the way they paused in their restless, graceful swirl.

"Tell us more." A swirling demand, five voices as one.

"Those who stood against the magician, those years ago. The humans. Their descendants sought to continue their work—and sold themselves to my master, to do it."

The swirl picked up again, disdainful. "That is your business, not ours."

The fabric of his shirt stuck to his skin, pasted by sweat even in the cool night air. "Ten men, my master claims." Nine who waited, and one who ran. "What would you do for an entire town? Yours to observe, to entertain you, without any cost to yourself."

"Ours? No cost?"

"My master cannot touch you, not here, not bound as you are."

That was not the same as no cost, but he was playing on their boredom, and their greed, to blind them. "An entire town, brought here, for the length of the lives of those who swore their oath," Jack said. "The natural life, and no more. When that last man dies, the town goes free."

Dying, bound to the rock... Jack did not know what would happen to their souls. But they would be unclaimed, and therefore not belong to the devil. Perhaps their god would intervene.

The swirling slowed, paused. He had their interest, now.

"Can you do this? Can you hold them to you, secure within the stone?"

He had his cards; he did not know what they held.

"If willing, we can."

That was enough. They haggled over terms for the rest of the night, Jack making them each one agree to every term. And when the moon set but before the sun returned, they had a bargain.

"They will agree? They will be bound?"

Jack shifted in his saddle, feeling his bones ache, exhaustion gnawing a hole in his skull. "They will have no choice."

The men were waiting, as he knew they would be, on the steps of the church. No children played on the planed sidewalks this time, no women gossiped in the stores, no youths recited lessons, or brought in the cows.

Briar waited.

"Is it time?"

Time, and past. He stared at them, from the back of the piebald. "What would you give, to stay with your family?"

"You make a joke of our fate?" The youngest spoke, his face pale and tight with grief, while the others stirred uneasily around him.

"I'm asking you a question." Jack's temper, unused to dealing with people this long, frayed thin. "Answer it, or be damned. Would you break oath, give yourself—and your families—over to a lesser evil, to keep your souls, and save them from heartbreak?"

It was too late to save them, too late the moment they made their deal. But there were different levels of damnation.

"Yes." Not the oldest nor the youngest, nor the speaker from the day before, but a slight, slender man with the look of a storekeeper about him, narrow faced with sideburns too large for his chin, and spectacles perched on his nose. "Whatever price, it cannot be worse than what we have already pledged."

"Nathan, be quiet," another man said. "There is always something worse."

A town of foolish men, but not fools, it seemed.

Jack, bluntly, told them what they faced. To go to the devil now in payment, or sidestep it, and hope the devil was amused enough to let it go.

"Decide now," he said, cutting off any discussion. "You who made the bargain must seal this the same way, else it cannot work. Ten souls bound, either way you go."

"We are only nine," Nathan said.

The oldest man, their leader, looked to Jack. "The devil's dog will deliver the last to his master. Will you not?"

Jack did not answer the obvious, but merely waited for them to decide.

As he had told the demons, they had no choice.

Nine men and their families, and the family of the tenth man, and the ties they had made; it was nearly two hundred souls and their households Jack led to their fate. Briar was left near-empty behind them, but it was a sturdy town, it would survive. And this time, Jack thought, they would know to lure a magician, and heed their town's warning.

Nearly two hundred souls, all of them willing, he led to the rock's spine, and delivered them to a different fate.

The hollow of the stone was barely a dozen feet long, and half that across. But it was large enough to contain them, and give them the illusion of land stretching beyond. A man's lifetime was only so long, even the youngest of them, and once the nine died, their children and children's children would be released, unstained by their fathers' folly. The devil would have no claim on them, body or soul.

The demon gathered above the hollow, stretched on their flat stomachs, watching the town rebuild itself the way humans watched a game of dice.

Jack, forgotten, gathered the reins and swung up into the saddle. Digging his heels gently into the piebald's sides, the pair moved down off the rock, and onto the endless plains. The devil did not hold a grudge. This one time, Jack had outplayed his hand, and taken the pot. But one game changed nothing: He had a missing man to chase down, and deliver unto the devil.

He thought he could hear the laughter, and a gentle *well-played*.

The devil demanded obedience, but there was give in his rope. If the Jack lived long enough, he could outride his own damnation.

In the Devil's West, only a fool asked for more.

Boots of Clay

I n his dreaming, they still lived in the village he had been born in, family to every side, and when he woke each morning, it was with the cold knowledge that all of that was gone.

Gershon swung his knees over the side of his bed, feeling cool wood under his feet, the scratch of rough wool blanket under his palms. One of the other beds in the cabin was empty, the other two still holding blanket-covered lumps. "I thank you, living and eternal one, who has returned my soul into me with compassion. Blessed art thou, who led us from fear and into this day, this Territory."

He thrust his feet into boots now, rather than the shoes he had grown up with, and they made a solid, still-unfamiliar noise on the doorframe. He reached up to touch the mezuzah as he passed, the battered tin casing a familiar reassurance.

This much, they had been allowed to bring with them.

Outside, the sun had risen over the treetops, filling the sky with light. He had gone to bed late, the stars thick-spread overhead and the howls of beasts in the distance all a reminder of HaShem's glory, but the expanse of blue sky overhead always surprised him, reminding him of the vastness of this land.

This strange, still-strange land.

The right to settle here had cost them seven chickens—bright-eyed, brown-and-cream feathered—and two cows born on the way from Pennsylvania, plus a bull calf come next spring in payment to the native tribe who lived there first, but the water of the creek was sweet, and the lands gentle and free from rocks. Even the forest seemed kind, although the last settlement, an hour's walk south, had warned them to use caution if they entered the woods.

"Their gods live there," Isaac had repeated, when the village was only an encampment of wagons turned inward, the men sleeping outside, starting awake at every unfamiliar sound. "And bears."

"I fear neither bears nor heathen gods," Yakob had returned, and the two had fallen into discourse on the nature of gods that might live in a forest, and if a correlation might be drawn between the tribes of this land and the tribes of ancient Judah, and if so, might they also be brought to understand Yahweh.

Gershon had left them to it; he had no Talmudic bent, no desire for an afternoon spent negotiating arguments that had little application to the moment, and he knew, of experience, that they would argue the matter until they had long ago forgotten the original question. They still, he assumed, had come to no conclusion.

But in the meanwhile, the wagons were dismantled, homes built, and a village had grown.

The community of Shaaré Tikvah was now seven months old. Through the grace of HaShem and careful planning, they had lost only one calf and Yosef Elder's three fingers to the cold, and now the wooden slats of the wagons made a pasture fence, and the blankets rested on beds under rude but water-tight roofs, made with the aid of Strong Knee's people.

He still had trouble thinking of this as home, but others had adjusted more easily.

"Good day, Gershon!" Miriam called, and he lifted a hand to acknowledge his cousin, her two young ones clinging to her skirts, but kept walking. His thoughts were too unsettled for prayer.

They had paid—everything they had—to come to this land, chasing a dream. They had been warned that this was a harsh land, but how could it be harsher than what they had left? At least here, they were promised, there was no Church, no auto-da-fé for those who refused to renounce their faith. The Territory worked on a simple principle, they had been told: give no offense. And if the wild folk of the Territory were heathens who worshipped idols and animals, if the creature who kept the peace here was called the devil by those who knew no better? The unknown was better than remaining like sheep to be slaughtered by the known.

Strong Knee had sent his people the morning after they arrived, unable to go farther, unwilling to leave this respite of open valley and fresh water. His warriors had eyed them carefully, circling around the small, clustered camp, and then disappeared, returning midday with venison and maize, skin blankets, and carved wooden toys for the children.

"You run from pain," Strong Knee had said. "You need run no farther."

They owed more than chickens and cows to their new neighbors. But how could one repay what was not a debt?

The first warning had come two weeks before. Two of Strong Knee's warriors had gone missing, their ponies returning, lathered and wild-eyed. Yosef Younger, Ham, and Abner had gone with the party to search for them, but returned empty handed, without explanation.

Men died. This was fact. But to disappear in such a way?

"It may be that another tribe took them." Horsehair

Boy had been one of the warriors to look them over that first morning, and become a regular visitor to Shaaré Tikvah, often sitting quietly while they prayed on the Sabbath, willingly fetching water or making fire as needed. The elders thought he might be willing to learn, but Gershon thought he merely found them curious, the way he might watch a new bird in the trees to better understand its song.

The natives spoke of their own gods, of the winds that carried medicine, the myths they spoke of as though of relatives only recently deceased. They had no interest in the prayers or beliefs of their neighbors. And yet, there was a familiarity to their faith that made the folk of Shaaré Tikvah ease their shoulders a little, speak less softly, sleep more deeply in the night.

Then one of the native camp's fields was ravaged, something churning dirt, trampling the soft green sprouts, and the young woman who had been on guard against night-grazers left with a headache and a lump on the back of her head.

Shaaré Tikvah's fields, smaller, closer to their homes, were left untouched, but within their walls there was murmuring, worries.

They knew, firsthand, that this was how it began.

Two days later, an empty storage hut was torched, the thatch burning bright into the dawn.

In the days after, the children of Shaaré Tikvah were kept closer to the houses, sheltered by the young women who carried hazel staffs, thick as a thumb, in unaccustomed but determined hands. An older boy, just past his mitzvot, perched on a roof with a ram's horn to hand from sun rise to set. At night, they barred doors and waited, sleep restless, riddled with memories.

And the men argued late into those nights, thoughtful, but heated.

"We have the right to call for aid. When we came here, we were promised that."

"From the devil?" Anton scoffed, frowning his disapproval.

"They call him that from ignorance," Yosef Elder said. "He is the power in this land, and we have given no offense, to be at risk."

"We are not at risk. Our neighbors are. It is their problem, not ours."

"If they are at risk, do you think we will not be, soon? They have no claim on the Master of the Territory, and we are far from others, far from this devil. He cannot protect us from enemies at our front gate."

Not in time, they meant. Not before their homes could burn, their belongings splintered and destroyed again. Everything they had built, gone.

"And how do you say we protect ourselves, then? Prayer? Or have you some secret training with guns or knives, to be our *militares*?"

They had been forbidden weapons back home; forbidden any means to defend themselves. The handful of muskets they carried along the journey were used for hunting deer now, and they had only a few bullets left. The women carried staffs, and the younger men had begun learning the bow and arrow, but they were not competent hunters, yet.

"We must distance ourselves from the village. Show that we are no danger, no risk to whoever threaten them."

"Abandon those who aided us?"

"This is their problem, not ours."

And thus it went, for nearly a week, until erev shabbat came, and the rebbe placed one weathered hand on the table between them. "We have eaten at their tables, slept under their roofs. They are our neighbors." Once the rebbe spoke, discussion continued, but the matter had been decided. Shaaré Tikvah would stand with Strong Knee's people. But how? They were farmers and scholars, not warriors.

Gershon had leaned back in his chair and watched the candles flicker.

Miriam and her younglings and the noise of the settlement now behind Gershon, there was peace. Birds chirped and trilled overhead, the grasses sighed at his feet, the sky arched over him with the blue promise of HaShem's lovingkindness. He could see Strong Knee's village in the distance, half a day's walk beyond, across the creek that served both.

That peace was an illusion.

Two nights after the rebbe's words, something destroyed the men's sweating lodge at the edge of Strong Knee's village, knocking an entire wall and half the roof down, as though a great wind had swept through, although none inside were harmed. Ham, who had a keen eye, had gone to look and found sign of metal hooks attached to the shattered remains.

Not a beast, then, nor an angry spirit or bitter wind, but men.

And from the works of men, there could be protection.

Gershon had gone to sleep that night and woken with the madness of a plan.

N ow, he touched his fingertips to his Tallit, feeling the fringe move gently. A prayer rose to his throat, but he stifled it, holding back the words. The creek rushed at his feet, the banks smooth with mud. It might not be enough; it would have to be enough. Shedding his jacket and his narrow-brimmed hat and placing them on the grass behind him, he rolled up the sleeves of his shirt, picked up the rough-carved wooden shovel he'd carried from the village, and began to work.

I t took him the rest of the day to gather the clay, mounding it in the sun to dry so he could clean it of impurities, then slaking it down again with river water. Living water, fresh and running; for this, rainwater gathered in buckets would not do.

The sons of Deer Walking appeared, as though drawn to see what the white man was doing, bringing him dried grasses and dung, watching with curiosity as he blended them into the clay, nose wrinkled at the sun-warmed smell. He had been raised with books and inks, not beasts, and while it was not unpleasant, it plagued the senses.

"You are making … a doll?" The older boy soon became bored and wandered off, but the smaller son, a bright-eyed child of seven, moved closer, fascinated by the figure taking shape under Gershon's hands. "A ceremony doll?"

"Of a sort." He had visited as well, his scholar's mind always eager to learn, and had some sense of the ceremonies their people observed, with dancing and cries and brightly colored cloths; it had reminded him of Purim.

"You are a …." The boy struggled to find a word in English. "A mystery-man?"

Gershon did not recognize the term, but the tone the boy used suggested meaning. "I am no hakham," he responded. "Not like our rebbe. I am merely a shaliah."

"Shal-leelah?"

"A go-between," he said, his fingers deep in the sticky clay, thumbs forming eyeholes and a mouth, bringing the excess clay back to form rudimentary ears. "One with authority to ask for things. To arrange things."

He had not asked for the role, but the weight of it had eased him, in the early days of their leaving. He could bargain, negotiate, ease the way. It was not the same, but it was something.

The boy scrunched his face, then nodded once, with confidence beyond his years. "A medicine worker. What do you do now?"

"It needs to dry in the sun."

"The sun is almost gone."

"And so it will wait until tomorrow. And you should be getting home for your chores, or else get no dinner."

The boy grinned at him and took off to find his brother, curiosity faded in the light of more immediate concerns.

Alone, Gershon considered his creation. Tall as himself, which was to say not tall at all, but broader in the shoulder, with heavy hips and arms that hung graceless at its sides, the face a smear of features, the cheekbones high and wide, the ears lopsided, the mouth a shadowed, lipless hole.

Gershon returned to the riverbank the next afternoon, heart in his mouth that something might have happened to the figure, that it might have cracked in the sun, or someone damaged it, beast or man. Instead, he found Deer Walking's youngest son sitting cross-legged next to it, as though playing sticks with a friend.

The boy looked up when Gershon approached, sunlight finding red in the blackness of his hair, his eyes bright with anticipation.

"May I watch?"

He was a child. A child should not be exposed to such things.

And yet, he was interested and eager to learn. Gershon could not bring himself to refuse such a student.

"Move back and remain silent."

The clay was warm and rough-dried to the touch, giving only slightly when he pressed a thumb into it.

Prying the half-dried mouth open slightly wider, Gershon reached into his pocket, and took out a tightly-rolled scrap of paper, carefully torn from one of the rebbe's books, fresh letters inked in the blank space.

This was no thing he should do, a reach he should not dare. And yet, the rebbe had tasked him with this; as shaliah, he could bind others to terms, could make agreements for his people.

His hand shook as he placed the tiny scroll into the figure's mouth and pressed the hole closed.

"My name is Gershon ben Adão, of Shaaré Tikvah of the Territory. I have been tasked with ensuring the protection of our synagogue from those who would harm it, and those who have given us friendship and shelter. Adon Olam, if you find these goals to be worthy, grant life to this most humble figure of mud and dung. Ain Soph, who caused Creation in your wisdom, grant spirit to this flesh, that it may protect your children, all born of Adam, though they know it not."

"You give it life?"

"Not I. I merely ask."

The boy nodded, more serious than a grandfather. "The winds will bring it life, and it will protect us?"

Horsehair Boy spoke of the winds thus as well, in tones of respect and caution. Gershon shrugged, stepping back from the figure, his fingertips touching the fringe of his Tallit, words of prayer gathering behind his lips.

The golem's eyes remained empty, its mouth pressed shut, its limbs clay without breath.

"Your will be done," Gershon said, and placed his hand on the boy's shoulder. "Walk me back to your village?" Because children had not been attacked did not mean they would not, but it would injure the boy's pride to suggest he needed a white man's escort home.

O n the riverbank, the wind shifted in the grass, and two fish splashed against each other in the creek. And when Gershon returned that evening to return the clay to the river, the figure was gone.

T hat night, he ate his meal with the rebbe's family. The old man was pensive, a single lamp on the table between them, the remains of dinner cleared away, his wife the rebbetizin shushing their daughter as they moved about in the kitchen.

"Why now? What here?"

The rebbe turned his hands palm up, a familiar gesture of acceptance, resignation. "Who are we to question HaShem?"

"Who are we *not* to question HaShem?"

That made the rebbe smile. "And did he not answer?"

No, Gershon thought, looking down into his tea. *Not the question I am asking.*

A runner came a day later, in the hour before dawn. He waited, panting slightly, while the men finished morning prayers. Unlike others, the runner did not exhibit impatience, but waited until ritual was satisfied and the rebbe came to speak with him.

"Sweeps Water would show you a thing, if you would come to see it."

Even in a hurry, Gershon thought, *they were polite.* It was oddly unnerving to those used to being ordered about, forcing them to question the intent behind every request, sifting through words offered sideways to see where the sword waited. Offer no offense, they had been told, as though their very existence had not been considered offense enough, nearly two thousand years now.

"We will come," the rebbe said.

B y "we," the rebbe had meant Gershon, who was younger and stronger and could walk more swiftly, and three of his choosing. Even so, the sun was well-risen by the time they came to where Strong Knee and the medicine man, Sweeps Water, stood in the debris, his ink-marked eyes narrowed, knees half-bent as though caught between a crouch and rising. Behind them, a young man Gershon did not recognize waited, his eyes more lightly marked, hair clubbed back to show a scar along his neck, livid and raw. An arrow, stung across flesh and half-healed. One of those restless young men, proving their worth by raiding other towns.

But this had been no raid.

They stood on the bank above the creek, the village too-quiet behind them, as though those within all held their breath. Even the dogs, rawboned and yellow-coated, lay still outside the doorways, waiting for humans to set things right.

"We heard them come, past moonset." Sweeps Water did not rise, but he was clearly addressing the newcomers. Abner and Ham shifted uncomfortably behind him, and Old Yosef coughed politely, waiting for the native to face them. Gershon did not bother.

"And they did this?"

"No. But you knew that already."

Sweeps Water did rise and turn, then. His skin was smooth, save for a cut through one eyebrow, but his hair grayed in thick streaks where it was tucked behind his ears, and the bare arm that gestured around them was corded with lean muscle and scar tissue. Gershon let his gaze follow the gesture, and wished he hadn't. What they had taken for debris was bone, flesh intact save where it had been severed, more like a deer's haunch than a human limb.

Once seen, it could not be unseen: too many parts to be even three or five men. Seven at least, perhaps more.

Ham gagged, bile rising and splattering on the ground as though he'd never seen dead flesh before. Abner muttered at him, shoving a kerchief at his mouth, then looked to Old Yosef, whose expression had not changed.

Old Yosef had served in the army when he was young; he had seen men die before.

"We heard them come, and we readied our arrows and our staffs. If this was to be a raid, we would meet it as warriors. But they did not enter the village. And then the screaming began." Sweeps Water looked at him then, and rather than the fear or rage he had expected, Gershon saw only exhaustion and sorrow.

Something acrid burned in Gershon's stomach. "Your village was not harmed?"

"None within came to harm," Strong Knee agreed, but his voice did not say this was a good thing.

"There is blood in the bones now," the young man said, and Sweeps Water shot him a glance that clearly told him he spoke out of turn. The young man did not care. "Spirits linger where the bones are blooded. And we do not know their families, to bind and release them."

"A thing destroyed them," Sweeps Water said to the men of Shaaré Tikvah. "You know of this thing."

Gershon forced himself to look at the remains of what had been men, once. "I do not know for certain." He had seen nothing, could say nothing for certain. The figure had been gone, but that did not mean it had walked on its own. "I asked our god for aid, to protect us. And our neighbors."

They had asked before. Endlessly, before, and the only answer had been in broken bones and burnt homes, in suspicion in the eyes of neighbors.

A muscle jerked in Sweeps Water's jaw, and something in his eyes changed. Gershon did not look away. "If in doing so, we have given offense in some way…"

The air stilled between them. He could offer no more chickens, no more calves, reminded once again how precarious their lives were, even here. Forever at the mercy of those who had no reason to choose mercy. Strong Knee had allowed them to build here, but Gershon had done more.

Would this home, too, be taken from them?

"The thing of clay you shaped. The creature of the bones and dirt."

Gershon swallowed, feeling the men behind him still once again, for different reasons this time. "Yes."

Sweeps Water studied him. "You worked medicine for us."

He had not; he had only petitioned HaShem. But Gershon merely nodded. What did the details matter? They had meant to help, had meant to share what little they had with those who had given them everything. He had not thought it would be unwelcome.

"This one was correct: the bones are blooded, and we do not know their names."

Gershon heard what was said: They could not honor those who had come against them. This land was beautiful, but it was strange, the people it made were strange, and his fingers touched the fringe under his vest, his lips moving in silent prayer that he might be given better understanding.

"This is gratitude?" Ham burst out, and Gershon turned to snap at him to be silent, but old Yosef's elbow landed in Ham's ribs first.

"Be silent, fool," Old Yosef told him in the language they no longer used in this place, the syllables odd under the weight of open sky and heavy pine, and as though summoned by it, Gershon felt the regard of something silent, measuring and thoughtful.

"It watches us," Sweeps Water said, and both Strong Knee and the young man at his side tensed: they had not felt it, either. Gershon did not look at the men behind him, afraid to break Sweeps Water's gaze, afraid to see what watched them from the shadow of the pines, hands wet with the blood of men.

"It is a guardian," Gershon said, searching for a word that would explain and finding none. "It will not harm you."

The other man's eyes narrowed, the dark markings around them only emphasizing his expression of—not doubt, but consideration. "So long as we do not harm you."

To live unharmed, unmolested, unthreatened. All they had looked for, coming to this new land. So many times before, they had called for help and been unanswered. Here, in this place, YahwehHaShem had answered. Gershon felt the weight of what watched on his skin, and his fingers fell away from his fringe. "I think ... it did not see a difference between us."

But there was. A vast gap, that all the good will in the world could not bridge.

Sweeps Water closed his eyes, his stern expression not slackening, but softening, slightly. As though he also felt what Gershon felt, both the weight and the gap.

In Strong Knee's face there was no suspicion, no anger; only sadness, and waiting.

"These grounds will need be cleansed." There was a command in those words, and a request, and Gershon bowed his head before them both, the acrid taste in his mouth softened by the faint mint of hope.

Two days later, Gershon returned to the creek bed. His shoulders and elbows ached, and his skin was bruised from kneeling, his Tallit fringe smudged with ash and soot from the offerings they had burned. It had been a small satisfaction when he saw how certain things rested comfortably against each other as they burned, rather than knocking each other aside.

Perhaps he was wishful; perhaps it was a sign. He was no mystic, to tell such things. But he clung to it, nonetheless.

Ashes into the ground and ashes into the wind. He would not compare it to the burnt offerings made at the Temple, in better days of better men, and yet he could not help but remember how the wind had swirled, dust sparkling in the morning light. Strong Knee's people were satisfied, Sweeps Water's eyes less shadowed.

But there was one thing left yet to be done. A thing only he could do.

"Bo elaiki anokhi yatzartikha. Come to the one who shaped you."

He waited, and it came to him, shoulders rounded

by weight, hands restless, but face implacably still, eyes dull and feet a dry shuffle. It came to him, misshapen by man's hands but glorious within. "Thank you," Gershon said, then reached into its hollow pit of a mouth, and with two fingers removed the scrap of paper from within.

The youngest son of Deer Walking found him there, hours later. The boy dropped to a crouch, small hands touching the lumps of clay where they had dried and cracked on the riverbank, as though something sloughed them off on its way back into the water.

"They argue, over the fire," the boy said. "Over what you did."

"I know." Gershon had not gone to the village; none of Shaaré Tikvah had, waiting once more to be welcomed, before they would presume.

"Sweeps Water spoke with the winds. For three nights. He has never spent that long with the winds before, and when he came out, his eyes were like an eagle's."

Gershon had no idea what that meant.

"It's gone now, isn't it? The thing you called."

The clay seemed to mock him, inert in a child's hands. "Yes."

"Many are angry. But Sweeps Water said that," and he was clearly repeating words he had overheard, "only fools refuse a hand that lifts them from the ground, or shields them from a blow. And that this guardian ... we might have need of it, again."

Gershon cast his eyes down, a prayer of relief releasing from his heart. "Then we will ask, again."

The boy considered that, thoughtful. "And if the answer is not yes?"

Gershon could only shrug, helpless before the Power that shaped them as the clay was helpless before him. "As AdonaiHaShem and the winds will it," he said.

A Town Called Flood

The way the story'd been told her, a preacherman came into town before there was much of a town at all, just the saloon and a couple-three homesteads, looked around, and pronounced that they'd be the first washed away, come the Flood.

The name stuck.

There were mountains not far off in the distance, and a creek that ran along the west edge of town, and a dozen storefronts and a bank, and thirty families living in Flood now. "Thirty pieces of silver," the boss called them, and would shake his head and laugh, and say they'd gotten that story all wrong, too.

The boss had a sense of humor. Not a man could say he didn't.

Come mid-June in Flood, the sun got hot and the ground was hotter, and mostly folk stayed inside or underground. June sixteenth, Isabel woke earlier than most and stood on the front porch, watching the sun rise over the far end of town. Main ran east-west, not north-south; the day began at the blacksmiths, and ended at the saloon, the scent of brimstone and hot metal always in the air.

She breathed in, letting the stink settle in her chest. Flood was the devil's town. He came and he went, but you could always find him there if you came callin'. And people did, even if they didn't always know they was looking for him. Back East, they called everything this side of the Mudwater River the Devil's West, but this was the only place he truly owned. Not the land, not the buildings, but everyone who came here, everyone who stayed.

"Izzy. What are you doing awake?"

She didn't turn around, but smiled, a gentle curve of her lips the way she'd seen the older women do. "It's my birthday."

"All the more reason to sleep in." The boss' voice was deep and smooth, gentle and oddly accented, even in this town where everyone came from somewhere else. In all her years, she had never heard him yell. Angry, yes: his temper was legendary. But he never yelled.

"I'm fourteen today," she said.

"Yes. You are."

He had been the one to draft her indenture papers; he knew what that meant.

She turned, and he stood in the doorway of the saloon, two tin mugs in his hands. The mugs were battered and dented, and tendrils of steam swirled over the tops as though an unseen finger stirred it. Chicory and coffee, and a chunk of sugarcane boiled with it.

She stepped forward and took one of the mugs, the thick dark brew sloshing slightly against the rim. "Thanks." He was the boss; he shouldn't be bringing her coffee.

"Not every day a girl turns fourteen," he said. "If you're determined to be awake, put yourself to use. Ree could use help in the kitchen."

She sipped the bittersweet brew, wincing as it burned the inside of her mouth, and nodded.

"And Isabelle?" he said before going back inside.

She looked up.

"Happy birthday, dearling."

She smiled then, for real, cupped her mug in her hands, and turned back in time to see the sun come full above the horizon.

Fourteen. Eleven years since she'd first set foot on

this porch. This was the only home she'd ever known; this three-story structure, the wide rutted street in front of her, the sound of the blacksmith's hammers and the bellow of cattle as they were run by town, the flickerthwack of cards laid on faded green felt, the clink of glasses, the scrape of boot heels on wooden planks, and the stink of sweat and hope and desperation on human skin.

Flood was home, the only one she could imagine.

But she was fourteen, now. Everything changed.

If she wanted it to.

Ree was already arms-deep in work when Izzy slipped through the open doorway, reaching for an apron hung on a hook to cover her day dress, a brown striped gingham with a cream yellow ribbon, special for her birthday. She'd threaded it that morning, and her hands'd been shaking.

Izzy prided herself on steady hands, and ordered thinking. She wasn't having luck with either, since waking. That irked her, and took some of the shine off the day. Having her name on the kitchen roster tarnished it some more.

It had been a cool morning, but the kitchen, running the length of the saloon, along the back, was steamy-warm already. Izzy didn't dislike working the kitchen, but it wasn't much fun, either.

"Knead dough," Ree said shortly, not looking up from his work. Ree was stern and mostly silent, but with an uncanny skill at getting every bit of flavor from some dish you'd swear you didn't like even as you were going up for more. He might've known it was her birthday or might not, and most probably didn't care.

Izzy tied up her hair under a cotton band, to keep the sweat from her face, and set to work. The dough was a sticky mass in a clay bowl, and soon enough her arms ached with the effort of turning it into something useful, but the quiet warmth of the kitchen and the repeating actions of her hands and arms were an antitdote to the tangle of thoughts churning in her brain

"Now leave alone."

Ree was talking about the dough. She'd been kneading longer than she realized. Izzy shook her arms out, wiping them with the warm cloth offered, and rolled her sleeves back down. She looked at Ree, frowning. His arms were covered with lines of ink, and he never covered them, not even when the wind turned bitter cold, and the horses grew their coats out thick.

"Why did you come here?"

She'd never asked, before.

Ree didn't say anything for the longest time, and Izzy thought maybe he wouldn't, until he did. "Nothing where I started, for me. Nothing out there for me. Here? Something."

She chewed on that a little, while she turned the dough into its resting bowl, covered it, and set it on the shelf. Nearly all the folk who came to Flood were looking for something, but most of them didn't stay. The town had a blacksmith, and a saloon, and they had a storekeeper and a doc who had two sons who did the grave-digging when needed.

If you stayed, Izzy thought, it was because the devil had need of you.

Manners were, you never asked what someone came for, and you never asked what they paid. She had gone as far as she could, and still be polite.

"Was it worth it?" The question slipped out anyway, like she was still a little girl who didn't know better.

Ree chopped a handful of carrots, shoving them off the board into the stewpot, every motion focused on what he was doing. If she had been rude, he didn't seem offended. "You deal with the devil, know what you want, and what you can pay. He don't ever take more than you're willing to give. "

How did you know? She wondered. How could you know what you were able to pay, and what did you offer when you had nothing of value except what he already owned?

Flood was his town. He owned everything—and everyone in it. Including her.

For one more day.

Her hands clean and dried, Izzy left the bread in its rising bowl, and wandered out to the window. Every room in the saloon had a window, except the back rooms, where the girls took customers. This one was small, and opened to the back alley; Ree tossed scraps out for the dogs, when he thought no-one was looking.

"What's out there?"

He didn't take her literally. "Beyond Flood? More towns. More people. Go East, there are cities. Lots more people."

"How many more?"

Ree looked at her, his eyes dark and unblinking, until Izzy started to feel nervous. She had known him all her life, it seemed, but just then he was a stranger.

"More people than you have ever met. More people than in all of the Territory, north to south. Too many people."

She had no basis for 'too many people,' the words were only words. "Have you seen a city?"

He shuddered. "No. No desire to."

She ran her fingers along the frame of the window, and looked out into the alley. If she wanted to, she could go to a city. Chicago, or all the way to Boston, or New York.

And do what, once there? Being a saloon girl—serving drinks and rolling cigarettes for the players, running errands for the older women who danced and fucked—was respectable here, but everyone said it was different outside of Flood, where the devil had a lighter hold. Nobody would protect her, out there. Nobody would care.

Ree sounded scared, by cities. Izzy couldn't imagine anything that frightening.

The saloon officially opened at 11, serving up coffee and whiskey to the men—and some women—who wandered in. The older women were still sleeping, but the male employees and the saloon girls were awake and ready, if they should be needed.

That morning, cool with early spring, the saloon was empty of customers. Christina, at ten the youngest and newest saloon girl, was sweeping the floor, while her brother, Christopher, polished the brass railing of the bar. They'd come over the winter, half-starved and terrified, dropped off by a stern-faced man with a marshal's badge. Their parents had been outlaws, and nobody else would take them, certain the twins would be trouble, too.

The boss had promised to beat it out of them before they were fourteen.

The Law respected Flood. Flood respected the law, in return.

Izzy sat on the catswalk that ran along the second floor of the salon, where the working girls lived, her feet dangling over the edge, watching the activity below.

The boss had beaten her, once. She had been their age, and mouthed off to a customer. The boss had laughed, in public, but that morning, when the saloon closed, she had been summoned to his office. Gavin, who had run the day to day saloon business back then, had assigned her chores to keep her standing up, that day.

Every now and again a preacherman came to Flood. He'd set up outside the saloon—never coming in, despite the boss's own invitation—and would preach for hours, sunrise to sundown, about how the devil was evil, the devil was wrong, the devil was a risk to their immortal souls, and ruining these lands, beside; that without him, the deserts would be green, the rivers lush, and no-one would ever die of hunger or thirst or Indian attack.

She had never been sick, never gone hungry, never been threatened by real danger—at most, a customer might tug at her braid, or pat her backside, until one of the older girls distracted him, took his attention back where it belonged.

She thought about that, and about what little she knew of the cities back East overflowing with people, and the lands even farther West, where the Queen of Spain held the coast, and kept the devil and settlers out, equally.

Her thoughts were still tangled, but she was starting to sort the threads.

Outside, the sounds of the town filtered in; voices raised in greeting, the occasional clop of hooves or rattle of wagons, a horse's neigh or dog's bark. Inside, it was hushed, the occasional scrape of a chair or clink of a glass, and the sound of cards in the boss's hands.

She looked down on him sitting at his favorite table, his hair gleaming dark red even in the dusty light, slicked back and curled, down to the turn of his collar, a neat goatee trimmed close against his cheek, his skin pale or dark depending on when you looked at him.

He knew she was watching him.

"What should I do?" she asked, not raising her voice a bit.

"Your cards, your call," he said, slicing open a new deck and spreading it out underneath his hand. "All I can do is wait and see how they're played."

The devil, contrary to myth, didn't cheat. He never had to.

Izzy sat on the balcony, her legs dangling in the air, and watched him. Supple hands, strong wrists, his shirtsleeves pulled back to show the sinews moving under his skin.

The working girls said he was a particular lover; only a few ever felt his touch, despite what the preachermen say. He liked women, he liked men. But he liked them adult, and willing. That was more than she could say about some of the men who'd come into the saloon. You knew them, the way they looked, the way they moved. You learned to tell, and evade, and not give them the chance to make trouble.

If they did, the boss gave them what they came for, and they never came back again.

"Tell me about my parents."

"They were young. And stupid." He says it without condemnation; stupidity is a natural state. "In over their heads and looking for a way out."

"But there wasn't one." She knew the story by heart, but liked hearing him tell it, anyway.

"No. There wasn't. They'd planted themselves in Oiwunta territory without asking permission, built themselves a house and had themselves children, and never once thought there might be a price to pay."

Everything had a price. Every resident of Flood

knew that. Everyone who survived a year in the devil's west knew that. "And then the Oiwunta came."

"They came back from the summer hunting grounds, and found a cabin in their lands, where the creek turned and watered the soil, and the deer had roamed freely. " He set aside the deck of cards, and slit open another pack, fanning the posterboards easily, frowning as he did so.

The backs of the boards were dark blue, pipped with silver. The last pack had been pipped in gold.

"They would have been within their rights to kill everyone within, burn the cabin down and steal all that was within." He paused, fingers splayed over the cards. "Although it's easier to steal, then burn. You never know what an Indian might do, though."

The natives didn't come to Flood, mostly; the boss said they had their own ways of getting into trouble.

"But they didn't," she said.

"They didn't. They'd been watching, the Oiwunt had, watching what happened elsewhere when the white folk moved in, and they were smart—smarter than your parents, not that it took much doing. The whites could stay, but they had to pay tribute. Just once, but something that would tie them to the land, tie them to the welfare of the tribe."

"Their child."

"Me."

"You." The boss shrugged, shuffled the cards and laid down a new hand on the felt, all his attention on the pasteboard. "They could have had other children; if they wanted to make a go of it out there they'd have to have other children, or hire help from somewhere else. But they were stupid, like I said. They refused. And the Oiwunta burned 'em out. Stole everything they had, but left 'em alive."

"And then they came here." Rosie added, unable to resist adding her piece. Rosie had been here then. Rosie, Izzy thought, had always been here, like the devil himself.

"To the Saloon?"

"To Flood," the boss said. "And, eventually, here."

Everyone who came to Flood came to the Saloon, eventually. To see, to deal, to press their luck, or to pay homage.

"Nothing but the clothes on their back and a single horse—and you, little mite all wide-eyed and closed mouth. Didn't say a word, even when your daddy handed you over." The boss chuckled, looking up at her. "Thought I was getting a quiet one. Proof even I can be wrong."

She remembered that. Her father was a hard-handed blur in her memory, and her mother only a soft voice and tears, but she remembered being handed over, the boss's face peering down into hers, and him promising that she'd never be sick, never be hungry, never be lonely, so long as she worked for him.

The boss kept his promises.

"What happened to them, after that?" She had never asked that question, before.

"They took the money from your indenture, and they left town."

"Where did they go?"

"West, to New Hispania. Or back East, maybe. No idea."

They weren't his; he didn't worry about them.

"**Y**ou thinking of following them?" Sarah was only twelve, and not a saloon girl; her mother was a working girl who'd decided to keep the baby, but Sarah followed the indentured girls around like a puppy. She'd come and sat down next to Izzy now, done with her day's chores, and not old enough yet to work once the saloon was open.

"Of course not," Izzy said. "Why would I?"

"They're your parents." Sarah's eyes went wide when Izzy shrugged. Izzy liked hearing the stories, liked imagining the house she'd been born in, on the banks of a creek with fierce Indians lined up outside on painted ponies like she'd seen sometimes, when Army riders went through. But the people who had birthed her had less relevance than the farmers and gamblers who came through Flood, and had left even less of a mark on her life.

"You gonna stay?" Sarah's voice was hopeful.

"I don't know."

A day to decide. At the end of her birthday, she would be fourteen for real. The term her parents had sold her into would end, and she could choose to sign on as an adult, name her own terms ... or she could leave.

The possibilities taunted her. Stay, and her future was decided. She would never be ill, or lonely. She could even leave the Saloon itself—some did, running errands or carrying messages across the plains and mountains, riding the rivers under the devil's brand, and the fact that she was a woman would make no difference—the devil had his fingers everywhere.

Leave, alone ... and everything was unknown.

The ones who left, they never came back.

By mid-afternoon, half of the six tables were filled, a few locals passing time and gossiping, a handful of strangers with the look of professional gamblers come to test their luck against the devil, and two who sat shoulder-slumped, drinking too slow to forget but too fast to be calm. One woman among them all, wearing widow-black trimmed with purple. That meant she was nearly out of mourning, or was out but decided black made her look exotic. Her dust-veil was tucked back, showing wisps of sin-black hair and a pale, square face that had never seen the noon sun, not without a parasol, anyway.

Men came to Flood for a hundred different reasons, the boss always said. Women only came for one reason: revenge. Izzy knew he would deal with her last, after the easier tasks were done.

She waited patiently for Po to refill the glasses, then carried them to the main table where the boss held sway, his hands sorting and delivering cards with nonchalance, as though gold and souls were not on the table.

Three men were playing that table, two sweating, one too cool. He was the one with the worst hand.

"What do you think, birthday girl? What do you see?" The boss's voice was scented with the cigars he carried but never smoked, and the lighter taste of the gold-colored whiskey he drank, a sip at a time.

Izzy knew what he was asking. "She's glad he's dead. There's something else she wants."

"A lover? Scorned, or unresponsive?"

"Another woman." Izzy didn't know how she knew that; something about the way the woman's head turned, the way she listened or simply how she wore her hat. "She hates another woman."

"Ah." He had already known, of course. But she felt a flush of satisfaction hearing his voice confirm her suspicion. People were so easy to read, sometimes. She finished delivering the drinks, and turned to go.

"And that gentleman, at the faro table?"

And sometimes, they weren't. Izzy studied the stranger from under her lashes, careful not to look directly.

Despite that, he turned, and looked directly at her. His smile was sly and sweet, and promised things she knew that she'd like.

"A charmer, that one. He's winning, and doesn't care." Most men cared, very much. Whatever they brought to the table they clung to—until they gambled it away in a moment of passion, and then the devil had them.

"Yes." The boss agreed with her assessment. "Why is that?"

It was a question, and an order.

I zzy ghosted to the man's elbow, her now-empty tray balanced on her palm, a saucy wink she'd stolen from Rosa in her voice. "You like a freshening?"

"That's all right, darlin'." He had a soft voice, faded around the r's and d's, and he didn't look up from his cards when she paused at his elbow.

"I can get you something else, if you like?"

He looked up then, and his gaze took her in, crown to toe. Izzy felt herself blush; there was no way not to, under such a look, but she made herself stand and take it.

He wasn't one of those men, but he looked his fill, anyway, and didn't seem to mind what he saw. "Your boss send you over to distract me?"

"If he wanted to do that, he'd send Molly, or Sue."

"Get me drunk then, drinking his surprisingly fine whiskey?"

There was good whiskey and rotgut behind the bar; Po decided what you got, no matter what you paid.

She let his wink go, and tilted her head at him, curious. "Why would he do that?"

"Why indeed? Because I've got a tidy pile of his house's money under my palm?"

Izzy almost laughed. "He doesn't mind that. The boss admires a man who takes chances, and plays them well."

"And to entice us in, he offers the only honest faro game in all the devil's west." His smile was cheeky, his dimples showing.

"The devil's house is an honest one."

"So I've heard."

She had his measure now: a cardsharp, a professional gambling man.

"You're one of his girls. Young for it, aren't you?"

"Fourteen." She put her hand on one hip, shifting her weight the way she'd seen Molly do, when she sassed a man.

"Young," he said. "But good bones, bright eyes, smart mind and a mouth that doesn't say half of what that smart mind's thinking. You'll be a handsome woman, soon enough."

"Handsome?" Izzy's pride was stung. "Not pretty?"

"Handsome's better than beauty," he said, leaning back in his chair, the cards under his fingers not forgotten but put aside, for now. "Lasts longer. Does better. A handsome horse, a handsome woman, they'll never give you grief. Pretty is heartbreak waiting to happen."

"That's a man's take on it. Beauty is power."

He laughed, and moved on his cards, proving he was watching what happened at his table, too. "Power is power. A good hand of cards, a bank filled with gold, a loaded gun, a pair of fine eyes and a bewitching smile ... the trick isn't what you've been given but what you accomplish."

He studied his cards, then studied her again with the same look. "A young girl with wits and looks could do well, beyond Flood."

"Is that an invite, mister ...."

"Matt. Matthew Jordan. You're a bit young yet for me to be offering any invites to, missy. But if you happened to be out front when I ride out, I would not be unwelcoming of the company. I've mentored before, not against doin' it again, for the right rider."

Izzy stared at him, her hand still on her hip, all sass forgotten.

"You mean that?"

"If you want it, girl, take it."

"Isabel. My name is Isabel."

"Isabel, then."

She stood behind the boss while he finished a game, and waited while the players took their winnings or left their losings. In the brief space before new players came, she gave her report. "He's a sharp, passing through. Wanted to see the how the devil's house laid down the cards."

"And he is satisfied?"

"Said you run the only honest game in the west."

"Hah. And so I do."

"He said I was handsome."

The boss skimmed her with his gaze, and smiled. "And so you are. "

"And he thinks I could do well, outside of Flood."

The boss put his cards down, and swung around in his chair. Izzy quailed inside, but stood her ground. He wasn't angry, just paying attention.

"You could. But not because you're handsome."

"Because you trained me well."

"Exactly." He turned back to the table, new players taking their seats, and she was dismissed.

I t was the devil's game, but he ran it honest. Mister Jordan had the right of that.

Izzy had lived in this room for seven years, since she earned a space of her own. There was a window that looked out over the front porch, directly into the top floor of the mercantile, a narrow bed that squeaked when she turned at night, and a chestnut dresser and a washbasin that had come all the way from the East, its bowl painted with green vines and tiny yellow flowers, and a wood-framed mirror set against the wall. She stood in front of the mirror now, the last tracings of sunlight gone, the room lit by the oil lamp that cast more shadows than light.

Sundown had come and gone. She was free.

Izzy took a deep breath, watching the dim shape in the mirror do the same. The stranger—Matthew Jordan—had come and seen something in her. Handsome. Strong.

"A young girl with wits and looks could do well, beyond Flood."

Mister Jordan had thought she was unhappy here, that she wanted something more.

Izzy untangled that thread from the knot in her head. She did want more: more than this room, more than serving drinks or servicing men.

Because you trained me well.

The boss had taken her in for four years, then indentured her for seven more, the work of her hands and back his at command. Clothed her, fed her, trained her...

"What do you see?"

He had trained her to think, to *look*. To see.

"Your hand, your call. All I can do is wait and see how they're played."

Bargaining with the devil is tricky, but he doesn't cheat. The devil takes nothing you're not willing to give.

If you're willing to give it all, that's not the trouble. Knowing what you *want* is the trick. You learned that, growing up in Flood.

You only ever get one shot.

When she opened her door again, the belowstairs was empty of customers, just the men stacking chairs, the working girls nowhere to be seen. Po cleaned the bar, polishing the brass, while Meggie racked the glassware, the clank and thud the same sound Izzy's heard every night for as long as she could remember.

Her parents had taken money, handing her over to the devil they knew rather than the red-skinned one they didn't. They'd abandoned her, maybe with tears and maybe not and it didn't matter, because she was Izzy now.

No. Isabel. Fourteen, and free.

A door opened and shut behind her, the wood creaking the way it always did, and feet shuffled past her, down the stairs. When they were open, everyone wore hard-soled shoes that tap-taped merrily on the wood. After hours, though, weary feet were cased in slippers, combed-and-plaited hair came down over shoulders, and tired faces smiled only when they wanted to.

Matt Jacobs would ride out tomorrow morning. She could be there. He'd mentor her, teach her how to survive—and maybe she could teach him something too, she who'd grown up in Flood, knew the flow of the devil's moods, his turns and his tells. She could become ... whatever she wanted.

Or she could stay.

Not to be a saloon girl, not to be a working girl. She had considered both, all the day, and rejected them. Serviceable jobs, decent jobs ... but she could not imagine herself in them. Could not see herself in those roles. She didn't like the kitchen, she wasn't much for the stables, not being a shopkeep girl.

Riding out gave her options. But the cities, with their people, their noise and bustle ... she couldn't imagine that, either. And the Spanish Coast was not her home.

This was her home. Flood. The saloon.

The knowledge rose up the way waters did from streams underground, sweating out of rock so quietly you didn't notice until you slipped on the slicked-down stone.

Isabel paused for a moment on the stairs, watching.

Rosie passed behind the boss, her hand touching his shoulder as she went, the same way she might pet one of the cats. He took no notice, but she knew he knows where they all are, every moment of every day. They were his, for as long as their contracts hold, and the devil never loses anything he cares to hold.

And he knows the things you don't even tell yourself.

He just waits until you figure it out.

The thing about the devil was, he knew there wasn't the one right answer. You were given skills, but it was up to you to figure out where they were meant to be. You had to test 'em all, see what fit. And when you did, he was waiting.

She could do any of the things she'd thought about. Only one of 'em was what she wanted, though. This was what she wanted, what she had been bought and trained for. To run the saloon; not now, but someday. To stand behind the boss and anticipate his game. To have power—That's what's she's meant for, what draws her. Not to explore, not to risk, but to control, to *run*. To help people get what they want, and have them owe her, maybe even crave her, in return.

He had known. Of course he had known.

He'd teach her, show her, set her free.

All she had to do was pay his price.

The Devil's Hope

There were seven crows waiting in the apple tree when Old Bear awoke. They watched him, beady eyes blinking, but did not utter a single caw as he stumbled out of the cabin, rubbing at his face and stretching sleep-tight muscles into wakefulness. Their silence was worse than their commentary; he felt the prickling of their regard between his shoulder blades.

He had slept poorly and woken too early, and was in no mood for whatever mischief they had in mind.

The creek still had ice on its surface, a thin crackling underneath which fat-sided silvers turned and turned, chasing tidbits as the waters drew them past. He broke the crackling, the weight of his shadow across the water making the silver fish turn again and scatter.

He cupped sharp-cold water in leathery palms, drawing it up to soften his sleep-parched throat. It was no replacement for another week or two of sleep, but there was no help for it. The winds had woken him, swirling about the rooftop and shoving cold fingers down the chimney, and if they were disturbed then he must be as well.

Considering the creek, he knelt, knees in the mud, and shoved his head underneath the water, feeling the bright coldness sting his skin. He pulled back, gasping, water dripping from face and hair, and shuddered.

Across the creek, a wary doe watched him, her belly thick with life.

"Get on with you," he told her, his voice scratchy with disuse. "There's nothing to worry about."

But even as she picked her way through the tall grass, he wondered if he'd lied.

One of the crows, more daring or more foolish than their siblings, spoke when he returned to the cabin.

"He is coming."

Old Bear glanced up into the tree, trying to track which one had spoken. Six of the crows fluttered their wings nervously, but the seventh stared back. "He is coming. What will you do?"

Old Bear growled, running thick fingers through the hair that clung to his scalp and neck, sending a fine spray of water into the sparse grass at this feet. "What do you care?"

The crow shrugged, which was no answer. Old Bear growled again, rubbing a damp palm against the flat of his face, before stomping back into his cabin.

He had woken and now he was hungry. There were beans in the pantry and dried corn still on the cob, and the lingering coals from the fire he had banked before pulling the blanket over his ears and going to sleep. It would have to do.

The crow followed him in through the single window, the tanned leather drawn tight and latched no match for its clever beak, while its kin shifted and hopped on the branch outside.

It didn't speak, now, but watched him, needy black eyes unblinking.

"I will do nothing," Old Bear said finally. "Not until he comes."

The crow tilted its head. "And then?"

Old Bear grumbled to himself, and said, "And then I will feed him crowbrother stew."

E ach morning for three days following, Old Bear
stood outside his cabin and waited, patient with
the knowledge that there was nothing to do but wait.

On the morning of the third day, he arrived, leading
a rawboned mule up the path, both of them surefooted
and sparse as goats. The silver shone on his lapel, proud
and pure, and Old Bear snorted even as he came to the
door and waited, arms crossed over his bare chest,
thumbs tucked into the curve of his elbows.

The man stopped a polite distance away, his gaze
taking in every detail of the cabin and trees.
"Graciendo."

"Marshal."

The man let a flicker of a smile touch his face before
becoming stern again. "You knew why I was coming."

"Did I?" He felt honest curiosity at the idea that he
had known anything, that this man might know what
he knew, that he might have done anything ever to
make a human come to his door, much less a human
bearing the sigil of the Territory, branch and root within
the endless circle. Perhaps he was still sleep-dulled,
perhaps more had passed him by than he knew.

The marshal pursed his lips, eyes dark as Old Bear's
own watching him from under the brim of his hat. "Are
we truly going to play the game?"

In the branches overhead the crows coughed their
mockery, and Old Bear sighed. "Come inside, then."

M arshals were a new thing for Old Bear, but there
had always been people on his mountain, for as
long as he could remember living there. For the most
part he ignored them, and they returned the favor.

Occasionally there would be a feckless cub seeking to prove his idiocy by venturing near to steal a clump of fur or a discarded shirt, and return to his fellows with proof. Depending on the season and his mood, Old Bear might allow him close, or chase him off with a roar.

"Old Bear is not tame," the Nuhwa elders warned their cubs, to no avail—if anything, it made them worse. But such was the nature of cubs, and Old Bear did not take offense.

There were others who made the climb as well. Elders in ceremonial gear, bearing offerings of dried fish and bread, sweet-smelling woods and carvings in his vague likeness. They left their offerings a distance from his cabin, retreating and waiting before making their requests, respectful without fear.

He enjoyed speaking with them, slow, thoughtful conversations that often left him more to chew on that the smoked fish or dried-berry leathers. Through them, he learned what went on beyond the mountains, in the long spread of earth that ran down to the waters.

It had been not too many seasons past when Braids Feet had placed a wooden platter on a rock, and waited until he had eaten his fill before speaking for the first time of white men at the banks of the Grandmother, and the being that rose up to bar their way.

Old Bear had thought at first he had misheard, and then that Braids Feet had listened too long to the moonfish and lost his way in their waters. "Who did what?"

"Was I somehow unclear?" Braids Feet was nearly as ancient then as Old Bear, and felt no need for polite words between them. "I will speak again, more slowly. A spirit has raised itself to stand on the Grandmother Waters, claiming mastery of the lands from there to here."

He had not misheard, and there was no madness in Braid's Feet's eyes that Old Bear could discern.

"A spirit." Spirits might meddle in the lives of those around them, for sport or purpose, but they did not take responsibility. They did not *claim* anything, much less the earth itself. "Master of the lands—and those who live within them."

Braids Feet inclined his head, metal-grey braid falling over one bare, bronzed shoulder.

"And you agreed to this?"

Braids Feet tilted his head back, grey-tufted eyebrows rising like an owl's. "It did not ask, any more than any powers ask."

Old Bear had to acknowledge the truth of that. Still, the arrogance, claiming the earth itself? He was not certain if what he felt was astonishment at the arrogance, or amusement. Perhaps both. But a claim of such needed power to hold it, either of winds or bone.

A touch of the bones beneath his feet returned nothing but a contented humming of sleepy winter turning slowly to growing spring; if this spirit had disturbed the earth with its claims, it was not yet apparent. Nor was there a sense of anything new within its bounds. And the winds remained silent, almost as though they too were waiting.

That was not a good omen.

"And what is it they seek to do, with this mastery?"

"For now, nothing. Shouting across the waters at men on the other side in the language of the southern horsefolk, until they left without crossing, and giving headaches to the medicine-carriers who live nearby. Their words to the People were gentler, but no less stern: if any man of white face is to cross the river, give him leave to pass, so long as he offers no insult, and gives fair trade for land he uses."

"And this being claims the right to enforce this?"

"It does."

"They seem to be young, yet," Old Bear said, a curl to his lip that had little to do with humor. "They may yet regret taking such bite, when it comes time to chew."

Braids Feet went away, and other elders came, other cubs came to count coup on Old Bear to prove their foolish bravery, and the seasons passed as they always had, Old Bear giving no more thought to the story Braids Feet had told, for what happened far away along the edge of the Grandmother Waters had little to do with him and his.

Until those who crossed Grandmother made their way father west, bypassing the fertile plains and game-heavy forests to climb into the jagged fingers of rock and pine where Old Bear made his home.

The first sounds had reached him on a crisp autumn morning, the crack and whistle bringing nothing good. He'd slammed the cabin door shut behind him, branches crunching under his heavy tread, the rumbling growl coming from his chest carrying forward through the thick-trunked trees. By the time he emerged into the new-felled clearing, his claws had emerged, pushing through fingertips and boot-leather as easily as plants pushed through leaf and loam.

He'd known what he would see, but it made the sight no less infuriating.

Voices exploded when he left the shadows of the tree line, shouting at him, around him, rising in pitch even as they raised their weapons, axe and pick and a single long-nosed musket.

He raised his growl to a roar that cut through their noise and cut them down as easily as they'd hewn the trees around them, leaving a stunned silence.

The men in front of him—filthy, clad in clothing that needed burning far more than the wood they had gathered, hair stringy, skin grub-pale under beards that rivaled his own—gaped in astonishment. Then one of them twisted as though to reach for the ax leant against a pile of rocks.

Old Bear growled again, and the man froze.

Not the People, and not the usual Spaniards, or even hunter-men down from Rupertsland tracking game, or they would have known better, with better manners. Five men in his sight, but he smelled more, the stink of urine and burnt meat, iron and alcohol. His nose wrinkled; the cubs occasionally stank of that as well, and it made them clumsy and loud.

"You need to leave," he told them in Spanish.

They glanced at each other, then one of them lifted his chin, face shifting from terror to stubborn determination. "What are you, to tell us what to do?" His Spanish was terrible, but comprehensible.

Old Bear snapped at the air, and gave the man credit for courage as well as foolishness when he did not flinch or run.

"We ... were told to dig here," the man said, his chin no less jutted for all that he still stank of fear.

"By who?" The others took a half-step back in reaction to his growl, and his ears flicked once and he rolled his eyes and lifted his paws, pulling the claws in as they watched. "I'm not going to eat you."

They looked to be all sinew and bone, even beyond the stink. He'd rather eat brambles and dirt.

"We made Agreement," one of the other men said, his voice shaking. "Agreement!"

Agreement. These humans kept bleating about Agreement, as though Agreement had anything to do with him.

His gaze moved past them, to the rough camp they'd thrown down overnight, grudgingly acknowledging that the shelter looked well-enough built, the fire pit rock-rimmed and cleared of debris, away from overhanging branches. He could not fault them there, though his beard twitched with the need to find something to vent his ire on.

"This place is not for you," he said in a low grumble, aware that they had offered no insult save foolishness, were no threat to anyone save themselves. "Get thee gone."

Unlike previous intruders, these did not flee at his command, but stood their ground, if nervously.

"We have the right to be here—" and then the speaker paused, one of the men behind him speaking rapidly in their language, a babble of meaningless sounds.

"Oh." The first speaker swallowed, blinked, the scent of him changing from fear and stubbornness to ... Old Bear sniffed the air. Embarrassment?

"We ... are you the keeper of this dirt? We have ... gifts, to give. That is right, yes?"

"No gifts. No camp. No you." His grasp on words was slipping, his face elongating again in his irritation, and he smelled sharper, fresher urine, as one of those before him lost control of his functions.

"We were told—" the speaker began again, his hand rising as though to push Old Bear back, and his temper, stretched too far, broke.

There was an unpleasant crunch of something in his teeth, the taste of grit in his throat, and he hoped that he hadn't bitten anything fatal. Rolling over, Old Bear felt the sun on his face, and the prickle of needle-leaf cushioning his back. He had not made it back to the cabin, taking refuge in a deep overhang. Licking around his teeth thoughtfully, he breathed in and out, feeling the faint hum of the earth below him, the bones of the world deep under the stone, pulsing in time to the rise and fall of his heart.

He remembered, vaguely now, the snap of teeth and the swipe of claw, as he'd broken the white men's camp, scattering stick and stone, dropping to all fours to prowl the outskirts, peeing on the marks of their presence, scattering the stones of their fire pit, until it appeared they had come and gone long ago.

Once they'd fled, he had no quarrel with them. With luck and common sense, they would flee far, and warn others that this mountain was not for settling on.

But luck and common sense seemed in small supply among these folk. Not a month later, when the streams were full-throated with snowmelt, he heard the sound of axes and shovels once again.

"Old Bear." This time the intruder stepped forward when he emerged into the clearing, rather than shying away. His Nuhwa was not perfect, but fluent enough to be understood, and his hand moved in the trade sign Old Bear had taught them generations ago. "We come with the consent of the Nuwa elders and the devil's advice, to bring the silver from the deep, that others may bend it to use. We have no desire to disrupt your peace, and offer no insult to your ancient self. Whatever gifts you require for our presence, we will do our best to offer."

The man spoke with the diffident straightforwardness of truth, and Old Bear found himself unwillingly paused. He felt the urge to tear them out of the clearing, to erase them from the land, but they had spoken fairly, without fear. He would give them that much respect.

"I do not know this devil you speak of, and I desire no gifts. You have nothing I need, nothing I've wish for." He wanted quiet, and solitude, and they could give him that only by going away. And yet. If they spoke true, and he thought they did, the Nuhwa had given them leave to be here. That was something new. What game did their cubs play at now?

There were eleven of them this time, well-formed men with the weight of hard work on their shoulders and hips. Their clothing rough and dirtied, but they carried themselves well, unlike thieves skulking in the night, and he sank to his haunches and waited for their leader to do the same opposite him.

"You plan to ... dig the earth, scrape at the silver?"

"Yes ...." The man looked puzzled, as though there was no reason to question their actions. Old Bear resisted the urge to growl.

He supposed he could, if he wished, understand the elders' thinking: Nuggets of pure silver were valued for their ability to warn of danger, to clear the paths and ease dreaming, and the mountains were stingy with what they let slip into the streams. Allowing these fools to disturb the mountains, while taking the benefit of their work.... Cunning, to use the Agreement to their favor. But no. He would be no part of this. If the Nuhwa had forgotten what would happen, he had not.

"You will die here, if you dig too deep. This land is not tame," no more than he was, "and it will not give up itself to you so easily."

"We know the risks, and the ... rewards." He used the wrong word, but Old Bear knew men well enough to hear what he meant. And he had listened, now, to what the Agreement required of the whites who crossed the Grandmother, who sought a place here.

His words were a rumbling growl, filled with intent. "I do not consent."

The man shifted, for a moment looking uncomfortable, but his chin was set and his eyes were hard. "The elders say you place no claim on this land. Your consent is not needed. We will do this."

Old Bear looked down at his hands, where the claws had quietly pushed through the skin. "You will not."

There had been more men seeking to dig the bones, and he had sent them away, but now a marshal sat by his fire, his long legs stretched before him, the dusty dullness of his boot leather a reminder that the road now led to Old Bear's door. And a marshal had protections against even such as he.

"Graciendo." The Spanish had named him that. It did not bother him, particularly; he had many names, and they all meant the same thing. "You can't keep doing this."

Old Bear looked at the marshal, and did not speak. He could, and he would. All they needed to do to stop him was stop sending fools here to die.

The fire cracked and popped, and the birds finished

their dusk-song, falling silent before the time of night-hunters. Something dropped onto the roof, a low, hollow sound, and then there was silence.

The marshal rubbed his hands over his face, then exhaled through his fingers. "Graciendo. You are ancient. And no-one gets to be ancient without also losing their foolishness. The Territory needs the silver the mountains hold."

"The mountains hold it for us." Parceled out bit by bit, carried in streams and rivers, not far, but far enough, and picked up and carried further in belts and knives, braids and boots, around necks and wrists and the ceremonial gear of societies.

"That worked when there were fewer of us. Better now that we control it, maintain it, than fools rush in and take it without understanding."

"Fools always rush. And end badly." He could still remember the taste of grit and gristle in his teeth, the feel of solid flesh under his paw, and wrinkled his lip at the memory. But he had given fair warning. The insult was not his. "Better to not let them near at all. Let them die somewhere else." Let them do damage elsewhere, far away from his home.

"My parents were fools once, too," the marshal said, his tone mild once again. "They crossed the Mudwater, looking for something they couldn't name, couldn't explain. It found them, taught them. Kept them alive until they understood."

The marshal's skin was pale, but he wore his hair like a warrior, and carried the sigil on his breast. Silver at his heart. He knew what he asked of Old Bear, knew what he asked of the mountain.

"These fools do not understand what they dig for." The blood of the bones was dangerous. Washed by the rivers, it calmed; taken from the birthstone, it shared a certain madness with the winds.

"Then *teach* them. That's what the devil's sending them for."

Old Bear blinked at the man, for the first time feeling a touch of surprise.

"Sweet River Jordan, you didn't...." The marshal lifted his chin, staring at the ceiling as though asking the winds for patience. Old Bear could have told him the winds did not know the meaning of the word, and even if they did, the price they would demand would be far too high.

"You thought I would teach them?"

"We didn't think you'd *eat* them."

"More fool you, then," Old Bear grumbled, feeling the skin under his whiskers flush. "And more fool your devil, thinking to send fools to dig the bones. Young or not, they should know better."

There was a flash of something in the marshal's eyes, a glint of sunlight despite the roof over their head, or the reflection of the fire, or something carried deep within, and then it was gone.

"There's no choice." The marshal's voice was deeper, darker than breath before, and Old Bear's head jerked up, eyes narrowing and nostrils flaring as though to catch the scent of something new-entered into his home. But it was only them; even the crows had left off eavesdropping and settled into their roosts for the night.

"More men will come," the marshal went on. "The devil can only keep them out for so long, can only filter their greed so fine. They crowd the shores, push their way in, spread and increase. It will happen, it *is* happening. The Mudwater is not enough, alone, to keep them out. The devil himself is not enough, not forever. They will come, and they will be too many to eat.

"The Agreement buys time, offers the chance to make them ours, rather the other way around. But we need to *use* that time."

Old Bear grumbled deep in his chest, fingers raking hair off his forehead, lingering at the back of his neck where a knot was beginning to form. He didn't like talking, didn't like thinking. He just wanted to be left alone.

"And bothering the bones? How does that better things?"

The look the marshal gave him suggested the man thought Old Bear was playing the fool. "Silver is power. More, silver is protection."

"You think I—"

"I think you see only what you want to see. What is comfortable for you to see." The marshal was still seated, still slumped in his chair, but there was a tension in his body Old Bear did not mistake. The sigil on his chest glinted in the firelight.

"The river and the devil will not hold them forever," the marshal repeated. "And you know what will happen then."

There was a stillness, even the fire pausing in its crackle, the settling of something thick and heavy in the air, sucking itself into Old Bear's lungs.

Deep in the bones, silver did not merely glint in stillness the way the sigil did. It flowed, living—and dangerous. To pull it, unwilling, into the air....

"Graciendo. For what is still human in you. Help us."

The marshal left in the dawn, his mule trailing behind, strands of grass still hanging from its mouth as it chewed.

"What will you do?" one of the crows asked, perching sideways on a branch, peering cock-headed at the figure below.

Old Bear let his face slip through, lips pulling back from teeth, snout wrinkling, ears flattening against his head, but the crow did not flinch nor fly off, waiting, attentive, for news to spread.

"The devil's hope is doomed," Old Bear said. "I'll have no part of it." He sighed, letting his face slip away, features smoothing back to facade. "But I won't eat them any more. If they've a hope, these humans, they will have the chance to earn it."

West Wind's Fool

G race Olcott stood in the middle of the road, palm sweaty around the handle of her bag, all her earthy belongings tucked within, and wondered what on earth she was doing.

"This is madness."

As though impatient with her hesitation, the wind belled her skirts and tangled it in her steps like an unruly cat, pushing her forward. She had only been cross-river for a handful of weeks, but already she knew to be wary of the winds, mercurial and magical in ways that made her skin prickle and her heart race unforgivably.

Wary, but not afraid. Fools died in the Territory, she had been told, and she was perhaps many things, few of them good, but no fool.

No matter what they had told her, back home.

Home. The word had always felt stiff to her, too ready to crack if she leaned upon it. It had not taken courage to leave everything she knew behind, despite what others said. Nor had it been foolishness, or desperation. She had simply woken one morning and understood that there was no reason to remain.

Everything after that had been simple logic: where could she go, that might be better?

West.

West was where you went when there was nothing else.

T he first leg of the journey had been uncomplicated, despite the sideways looks and quiet murmurs that greeted her at every stop. She had cast her eyes down and kept to herself, two decades' worth of learned quiet protecting her from overt censure; they could not scold what they would not notice. The second leg had been even simpler: the French had only recently abandoned their holdings in the wake of the war, and the remaining inhabitants of those half-empty towns seemed more worried about incoming British rule than who might be passing through.

And the closer they came to the River, she noted, the fewer sideways looks there had been, at all. Those who lived and worked along the Mississippi's banks were accustomed to oddity, she supposed, and those who crossed it … well, they were odd in and of themselves.

She didn't mind. She was odd, herself.

They had to wait two days in the small fort on the banks of the river before the captain would ready a crossing. She had watched him, testing the winds each morning as though the smell of it could tell him something, until he was satisfied, and the slender green flag was run up a pole to alert those waiting.

There had not been many: she had been one of only three passengers on the flat, unwieldy craft that carried them across; the other two had been men, aged and rugged, who kept to themselves, hands in pockets, staring at the far shore as though afraid to look back.

She had not looked back either.

When she'd paid her coins, the captain had eyed her carefully, and she'd thought for half a breath that he would refuse her fare, but then the coins had disappeared into his case, and his chin had jerked in the direction of the boarding ramp.

Neither captain nor crew nor her fellow passengers spoke to her during the passage, but as the tow-ropes were hauled in and tied to wooden stumps on the other side, a hand come down softly on her shoulder, hard fingers gripping the fabric of her dress.

"Sir?" She could remember her manners, even when those about her had discarded them.

"Beware things uncanny," the captain said, not meeting her eyes. "If you're bound and determined to do this."

He had not explained what he meant nor waited for a response, but took her bag from her without courtesy, tossing it to a man on the shore who caught it with ease. And then there was nothing for it but to follow, stepping off the wooden planks and onto strange new shores.

"Welcome to the Landing," the man with her bag said, his cheerfulness almost offensive in contrast to the captain's brusque behavior. "Head on straightaway, they'll sort you out."

The Landing was barely worth the name, despite obvious years of use; a half-circle of road leading to a plain hostel with a handful of rooms and a single clerk who did not bother to write her name down before telling her a room number, a mercantile for purchasing whatever goods might be needed, either overlooked or lost before arrival, and a livery stable where one might find a horse, or cattle to pull a wagon, also for sale through the mercantile.

She was the only woman to be seen, from dock to hostel. She had known—had suspected, from the stories—that this would be so. The men loading a wagon mid-street glanced at her, then went back to their work without comment. Civilized men on the other side of the river had behaved worse.

She left her bag in the hostel room, washed her face

and hands in the basin, and then stepped back out into the dust and quiet bustle. She bypassed the mercantile and instead leaned on the fence outside the livery, where several beasts were grazing the sparse grass underfoot, waiting until someone came out to see what she might want.

When they did, she learned that the cost of buying new was twice that of the obscene price charged to ferry a wagon across the river, but she had expected nothing less. Nor was any horse for offer worth the silver they were asking: those that had been sound once were now old, and the young ones already swaybacked or mean-eyed. The sole mule they offered had lashmarks on its flanks that spoke of either mistreatment or mean temper, and neither was something she was prepared to accommodate.

Grace was in no hurry, no rush to arrive anywhere. She could wait.

She extended her stay at the hostel, shaking her head at every offer she received, both polite and less so, until a family of seven invited her to join them when they rode out. She had observed that they were quiet folk, not prone to conversation, and wanted her only to help with the chores, not for her company.

She said yes.

The family was heading west and south, to where they'd heard there was good farming. Grace learned little more of them than that, and did not offer anything of herself—nor did they ask. The three older children walked with their father, the mother and two babes-in-arms resting in the wagon. Grace held one of the babies when it was given to her, awkwardly competent, then took her turn leading the cattle.

Her hands slowly hardened in new places from the slip of leather through her fingers, her forearms aching with new muscles, the bump and rattle of the wheels over rough road leaving her head sore when they paused each evening.

Slowly, they moved further away from everything they had known.

The days were long and exhausting. Meals were simple things, and at night the children and woman bundled themselves inside the wagon, while she and the man slept outside. She could have slept within, she supposed, but the cold ground was more than compensated for by the sky spread out overhead, purple-black clouds obscuring the changing shapes of the moon, the shadows lit by more stars than she had ever imagined before, and one night, a bright plume of fire that crossed the sky, causing her to gasp.

The man slept through it all.

Mornings, her back ached and the fabric of her clothing became soiled with dirt and sweat; the water they had was for drinking, and the streams they passed were too shallow and cold for bathing. They saw no-one as they traveled save deer they had not the skill to hunt, and rabbits they did, heard nothing save the susurration of the wind as it ripped past them, and the eerie calls of things hunting, or being hunted, at dusk and dawn.

The stories she'd heard, the warnings she'd been given, fell flat under the unfolding truth. Rather than the hordes of savages roaming the land, or the bountiful farmlands wanting only people to populate them, each day brought nothing but wide, rolling hills and rocky outcroppings, the sky spread out overhead either pale blue or brilliantly black, and the only living things they encountered carried on four legs, or two wings.

Grace would have found the emptiness peaceful, save that with each day the mother grew more and more fretful, the children more wild, and the man unhappily caught between them, until she thought she might smother them all in their sleep simply for a moment's peace.

She did not say any such thing, did not let her irritation show. It would be different here, she told herself. It had to be different here.

She slept less well each night, and woke more sore, less content.

And then one day, they came to a place where a fainter trail crossed the one they were on. The father stopped them, pausing a moment.

"Crossroads," he said, as though that meant something.

Grace stood beside him, and looked curiously at where the trails crossed. The wind lifted itself around her, prickling her skin. Behind them, the cattle balked and complained, and she turned her head, eyes straining to see something on the horizon that was not there.

Something scratched within her, faint and hot.

Uncanny, she thought, and then, *why not?*

She gathered her few belongings, and stood by the side of the road, watching as they moved on, the older children turning to wave farewell.

"You're certain?" The man seemed hesitant to leave her there, or perhaps hesitant for her to leave them.

"No. Not at all." She did not give him the smile she

had perfected over years, but a new one, pushing to her surface like something green in spring, and he blinked in the face of it. "But it will be fine."

They left her then and she felt the fabric of her dress shift around her as though a breeze tangled there, although her skin felt no air cooling the sweat from the noonday sun overhead.

The narrower track that had intersected theirs cut a path northward through tall grasses. The dirt was pitted and worn flat, and yet there was something about it that suggested a road less traveled, a path overlooked, or one that perhaps was not entirely there.

As though it had not existed before they rode up, and would disappear again if she walked away.

She shook off such fancies. Whoever walked this way went on foot, or horseback, not by wagon, and so left a fainter trace, that was all.

And yet, there was something about it that made her skin prickle.

Beware the uncanny, she had been told, but in a land reputed to be ripe with the uncanny, how could such caution even be considered? If she had embraced caution, she would have been still in her mother's house, preparing supper, or darning clothes, or some other practical, useful thing, making herself fit what was expected. Bending herself into a shape that was known, safe.

The very opposite of uncanny.

The smile she had given the man broadened into the grin her mother had more than once, despairingly, called feral. She lifted her face to the sky, eyes closed to better feel the light on her face. Then her knees bent and her boots lifted, and she walked down the center of that narrow, dusty road as though to dare anything to dissuade her.

W ithin a few strides, the first road was lost to view, and she did not look back again. Her path lifted and declined, a fierce stream interrupting its passage at one point. She eyed the running water cautiously, shifting her bag as though to gauge how well the tapestry cloth might fare were it to be dropped into those clear waters.

There was nothing for it: the wagon was long gone by now, even if she were to turn back, and there was no way forward save though the stream. With a deep breath, she stepped into the sandy waters at the edge, finding a shallow bridge of stones underfoot, slick but not slippery and enough to carry her across with dampness rising only to the ankle of her boots.

"Almost as though it wanted you to cross," she said to herself, as she reached the sandy bank of the other side.

"Almost as though."

She turned swiftly, her hand reaching for the knife she'd bought before beginning her journey, cold fury at having been crept up on filling her throat.

But there was nothing there. No human shape watching her, no four-legged beast, nothing save the shape of three birds far overhead, turning and turning in a widening circle.

She let her hand drop from the blade's handle, achingly aware that she had little sense of how to use it, save to cut things already dead, and tightened her other hand on the handle of her bag, aware of the weight of it. She would have better luck using it as a weapon to knock an assailant out than trying to defend herself with a knife.

An echo, that's all it had been. Some trick of the wind and water.

"Uncanny," she said, and for a moment, she thought she felt fear.

Suddenly, she was aware of how very far away she was from her home, much further than merely the miles she had traveled. But then, that had been what she had desired, had it not? To flee the confines that had pressed at her throat, pushed and pulled her into shapes she could not naturally form.

And if she met her end here, on a dusty deserted road in the middle of the uncanny wilds, well, that at least would be a more interesting fate than spending the remainder of her life trying to be what she could not.

That was what she told herself, as she shook the last drops of water from the hem of her skirts and tips of her boots, and looked up the hill in front of her.

Some, she had learned, crossed the river out of need or desperation, their past lives in ashes behind them. Some came in hope, thinking to make their fortune in some way, become something greater than they could be in the States. And some, like her, had no reason driving them, no dream or fear or incentive to leave all they knew behind for the unknown, save a thought that somewhere else had to be better.

And here she was, with wind at her knees and a lightness in her chest that had no explanation she could muster, only that they both lifted her, and carried her forward.

"One more hill," she told herself, although she had no idea if that was true or not. "One more hill to go."

I t was, in fact, two more hills, and the road flattened, revealing the checkmarks of fields in the distance, the blue-green ribbon of a river curling through the flat-bottomed valley, and between them, at the end of the road, a cluster of unprepossessing buildings, and the faint stink of something bitter yet not unpleasant in the air.

The breeze pushed behind her knees again, and she let it, her stride long now that she knew her destination.

S he had no sooner crested the final hill than the wind dropped off, an odd tingle running through her skin as it disappeared, leaving the fabric of her skirt suddenly heavier against her legs, the faintest hint of laughter echoing about her ears. But she had no chance to wonder at it, the road flattening out for the final few lengths into town.

Assuming one could even call it that. She sniffed once, stopping to consider the structures in front of her.

Once she left Connecticut, she'd not expected to see another city, and the towns she had passed through had been small even by those standards. But what was ahead of her could barely even claim to be a village. Five buildings set along a single street, all of them made of weathered grey lumber, as though whitewash had never been heard of on this side of the river. They were low-slung and battered, with none of the bits and bobs most folk set out around their homes; no trim or flowers, not even a rocking chair on the porch of the single building that had one. There was a blacksmiths' chimney smoking at the far end of the street, the black smoke the source of the odd tang in the air, like rotted eggs, dipped in honey. Her nose wrinkled again: how could they live with that smell in the air?

Still, she supposed it was no worse than the mills back home, and people became accustomed to those as well. But she wondered what metals the blacksmith worked with, that his fire caused such a stink.

"Not silver, certainly." He father had taken her to a silversmith's once, in New London. The smell of heated metal had been bitter, but a greenish bitterness, like raw onion, not this.

Already the smell was fading, and she thought that without the wind, it might not be so bad after all.

That settled, she took a second look at the town. It was small, yes, but the buildings were not quite so isolated as she'd first thought: there was a path coming from the other side that she'd missed before, that presumably led to the farms beyond. She noted it now only because someone was coming down it, pulling a three-wheeled cart behind him. His head was bowed low with the strain, and she wondered what he was bringing, and from where. Produce from one of the farms in the distance, maybe, but for what cause? There could be no market here, so far from everything—

She stopped and laughed at herself. Everything here was far from everything. But a market day would fill an empty square with dozens of people, easy enough, even if they had to ride for half a day to get there. Surely such a thing happened even here, in this great emptiness.

"Sir!" she called out when the man had come close enough to hail politely. He stopped, and looked up, revealing a dark face under the brim of his hat, and she almost swallowed her tongue in surprise.

He was old, too old to be pulling that cart by himself, and she felt a flash of anger at his master, that he would send this old man to do such a thing.

She caught the anger with long practice, smothered it and scattered the ashes.

"Excuse me," she asked finally, when he simply stared at her. "What town is this?

He blinked, sucking on his teeth thoughtfully, before telling her, "You've come to Flood, Miss."

"Flood." She thought of the river she'd seen, far too distant to reach here, and felt her brow furrow. "As in Noah and?" A Biblical name seemed … unexpected, at best, from what she'd heard of the Territory, but she did not know what sort of folk right have come here, first, to have the naming of their town.

Her question seemed to amuse the old man, his teeth flashing in a grin, the wrinkles in his face deepening around his eyes until they nearly disappeared. "Of a sort, yes, of a sort. But you'll have to speak to the Old Man to get the full story, iffy' you want it. He's the one who picked the name, as it were."

"The old man?"

"The boss." His grin deepened, a flash of mischief she hadn't been expecting. "You'll be wanting to see him anyway; nobody comes here first time unless they've business with him anyway."

"I'm not entirely sure why I've come here," she said, struggling to regain control of the conversation, but that just made the man laugh, a low, deep sound of amusement.

"Same reason everyone comes to Flood, I wager. Go, talk to the old man. He'll sort you out, one way or t'other."

"And he would be found … where?" She hoped that he wasn't the blacksmith; she wanted to get no closer to that stench than she could avoid.

"The saloon, miss." He pointed with his elbow

toward the two-story building. "He's always at the saloon, excepting when he isn't."

"A saloon. Lovely." She nodded once at the slave, and set her jaw, preparing herself for whatever lay ahead. Behind her, she could still hear him chuckling, and it only made her spine straighten even more, until her shoulders ached with it.

There was no sign posted on the building she had been directed to, nothing to indicate what its purpose might be. Then again, she supposed there was no need, in a place this size.

She had never been in a saloon, had never even been near one, far as she knew: there were alehouses back home, of course, but a saloon was a different thing entirely, wilder, far less respectable, one far less suitable for a woman, young or otherwise, to be entering.

Then again, she told herself, pausing at the first of two steps onto the porch, she had gone cross-river, and there were some—many—who'd say she had no claim to respectability any more. Or that she'd ever had it at all, save as a courtesy to her mother. What had she to lose, entering a saloon in a barely-there town, in the emptiness that was this land? And how terrible a place could it be?

She stepped onto the porch, bracing herself to open the door. But whatever she had expected, it hadn't been for a lean, nearly rawboned woman to open the door before she could touch it, robed not in scanty attire, but a sturdy, utterly respectable brown dress, her hair up in a braided coronet, her face free of paints or blandishments.

"You're early," the women said, "but not so early we're not open. Come in."

Whatever she had half-expected—drunkenness, lewdness, smoke and deviltry—it was not what she encountered. Instead of disrepute, the space inside would have made even the most scrupulous of housewives sigh in pleasure. The wooden floors were scuffed but clean, the walls lit with brass sconces that gleamed with polish, and the great winding-clock by the staircase looked as though it might just have been unloaded off a ship direct from London.

Inside, the entire first floor seemed to be filled with gaming tables, the surfaces covered with green cloth, surrounded by straightback chairs that couldn't be as comfortable as the men—and a woman, she noted with surprise—sitting there made them look. Only one table had a game going, the cards making a *flickerthwak* noise as the dealer turned them over; at the other table, two men seemed intent in a discussion that required a great deal of hand motions. She recognized the posture; they were likely arguing politics.

Even here, it seemed, some things remained the same.

"You here to test your luck, or just to see if you have any?" The woman had closed the door behind her, and was watching her now, arms folded over her chest.

"Luck is for those who prefer not to work," she said with some asperity, and the woman laughed at her, shaking her head in obvious amusement.

"Not in the Territory, it's not, but that's not a bad attitude to start with. What's your name?"

She opened her mouth, and stopped, tongue already forming the shapes. She had been asked that at the hostel in Landing, and she had given her full name, out of habit. When she had met the family she'd traveled with, she had done the same, as had they.

But there was no need, not any more. It was an odd realization to have, that her name, her family name, meant nothing here, now. No connections to be delved, no expectations to be upheld. Only her.

"Grace. My name is Grace."

The woman's eyes were kind, she thought, even though she was still laughing at her.

"And that's also a good name to start with. Welcome to Flood, Grace. Come, have a drink with me while you wait."

"Wait … for what?" She didn't care for spirits, but followed the woman to the long, polished wood bar nonetheless.

"Two, please, Iktan."

The man behind the bar was only a few years older than her, at a guess, bronze skin taut over a broad jaw, long black hair just starting to silver. His eyes were dark as jet beads, but unlike everyone else she had met so far, he did not laugh at her, square face without even a hint of mockery as he poured two drinks from a frosted pewter pitcher and placed the glasses down in front of them with a precision she could admire.

"Just lemonade," the woman said, catching her eyeing the glass suspiciously. "You don't seem the sort to need liquor to steady your nerves."

Grace still had no idea why her nerves would need steadying, but the lemonade—lemons, here!—was fresh and cool and perfectly tart, and she hadn't realized how thirsty she had become on that walk before the liquid touched her tongue and throat.

"That is very good," she said, placing her glass down carefully, hearing the clink of glass against wood, even over the sound of the card-players behind them. Her nails had grown too long and ragged, she noted, and there was dirt under them she had not been aware of before. The thought of a long, warm soak in a bathtub was a sudden craving, and she coughed once to dislodge it. "But if I may ask—"

"You may ask anything here," the woman said, and there was an amused cast to her face, although she was no longer smiling. "That is why we are here."

And that was the very first question. "And what is 'here?'"

"Flood."

She narrowed her eyes, suspecting that she was still being teased. "Yes, I know that, I encountered a slave outside—"

The woman coughed as though surprised, but recovered quickly. "We are not free, in the Territory, but neither are we slaves. Not any of us."

"Oh." She wasn't sure what to do with that statement, so vehemently offered, so merely tucked it away for later. "Well, he told me that this was Flood, and that I should speak with … the Old Man?"

The woman nodded, her lips pursing. "The Boss, yes. It's not a requirement, or anything of that sort, but most folk who come through here, that's why they come. Even if it's not what they do."

Exasperation won out over caution. "Does no-one in this land speak directly?"

The bartender did laugh then, a dry crackle of noise as he leaned on the bar, ducking his head toward them. "I like this one," he said. "She smells of the wind. I hope we keep her."

"Hush," the woman told him, and set her own drink down with a less delicate clunking noise. "But if you have been wind-touched, and Iktan would know, then you definitely need to speak to the boss. Wait here."

The bartender—Iktan, an odd name to match his odd face—refilled her glass before it was empty, and she nodded her thanks. He seemed disinclined to speak further, which she appreciated. It was not that she disliked people, or speaking with them, but she'd learned that tolerance for her oddness could turn to upset, too easily.

It might be different here. But it also might not.

Turning in her seat, Grace watched the business of the saloon.

Although the bar took up much of the long wall, it was apparent that drinking was not the main purpose of this room, but rather, gambling. There were five felt-covered tables, each with six chairs set around them, and placed so that there was space to move without jostling a player's elbow. She tried to imagine the room on a busy night, when every table was filled, and thought that it must become quite noisy and not a little overwarm. But for now, the air was comfortable, and the unpleasant tang outside was replaced by the more soothing smells of fine leather and tobacco, and an unfamiliar musk.

She sniffed, trying to identify the last, and thought it might be an undercurrent of the smoke from outside, but tempered somehow. It was … not-unpleasant.

The soft, dry sound of cards being shuffled drew her attention again, and she studied the one table currently in use, where the players were intent, occasionally tossing a card down or moving a coin from one pile to another. The faint glints of silver reminded her of the coins in her bag, tucked into an inner pocket so as not to jingle and draw unwanted attention. Silver coins, not paper money, the surfaces plain and the edges flattened, the easier to cut in half, or quarters. The mercantile at the Landing had had a pair of shears at the counter, and trimmed bits off her coins for the few things she'd needed to buy. It was a practical system, she supposed, but difficult to transfer any great wealth.

Then again, she thought as she watched the bits of metal move from one owner to another on the table, people did strange things with great effort, every day, and seemed satisfied with the results.

The two men at the other table had been joined by a woman, her gown more of what she had expected to see in a saloon, a shimmery green fabric that clung to her body more like a chemise than anything to be seen in public. And yet, it covered her shoulders and bosom decently, and her hair was respectably bound in a braided knot atop her head. The men spoke to her as though an equal, listening to her words with their heads inclined, their hands wrapped around mugs of something steaming hot, nodding or shaking their heads occasionally, but not interrupting.

Her father had listened to her like that, though he'd too-often ruined it by patting her on the cheek after, and telling her she was a smart girl, pity about that. She should miss him, she thought. She was aware of being gone from them, him and her mother both, but the sensation of absence was not, she thought, the same as *missing*.

She did not feel the same as other folk. Did not behave the way they did. But she had learned to pretend.

There were others in the room, she noted now that she had a chance to take it all in. A slender, well-dressed young man with pale blond hair lounged against the wall at the far end of the bar, watching the players. She studied his face, deciding that he was there to catch

anyone cheating. At the other side of the room, a young
girl wrapped in a white apron that covered her dress
near-entire, her hair in a chestnut plait down her back,
was arguing quietly with an older man in vest and
sleeves, until he threw up his hands and shooed her
away with a grin, only to have the woman she'd spoken
to earlier approach him, laying a hand on his elbow.

Was this the old man they'd all be speaking of? He
did not look at all old, though she supposed it might
have been a term of affection, or respect. His hair was
the same chestnut as the girl's, though threaded with
silver that glinted in the lamplight, and his dark-
complexioned skin seemed unlined from this distance.
She might have thought him only a few years older than
herself, if she'd met him at a social occasion.

He looked up at something the woman said, and she
knew that he was looking at her, though he did nothing
so gauche as stare. Then he nodded and turned away,
the woman's hand falling from his arm as she watched
him go. And then he ... simply wasn't there.

She blinked, but no. Everyone was exactly where
they'd been, save him. She looked down accusingly at
the glass in her hand, but she knew the taste of spirits,
and there had been none in her drink.

"Come on, then." The woman was back, looking at
her impatiently. Did everyone move so quickly, that she
could not see them?

Uncanny. The land—and the people as well, she
supposed.

She placed her glass back down on the bar with a
nod of thanks to the bartender, and followed the woman
in the brown dress through the room until they came to
the far wall, and a doorway she would have sworn on
her mother's Bible had not been there before.

"Go on," the woman said, pushing the door open a

crack. "You've made it this far, no reason to fear the rest."

The door closed behind her with a gentle click, and she was alone in a dark-paneled room.

No, not alone. The man she'd seen before was seated at a wooden desk. There was a single chair set in front of the desk, and she lifted her chin and walked over to it, settling her skirts carefully as she sat down.

Only then did she realize that she'd left her bag, with all her coin, all her belongings, back at the bar. A moment of panic fluttered her chest.

The man looked up from the paper he had been marking, as though she'd made a noise, and shook his head with a faint frown. "Nobody will touch your bag," he told her, and there was such certainty in his voice, she felt herself calm without second thought.

"Welcome to Flood," he said. "And to the Saloon."

"Thank you," she said, because it seemed the polite thing to do. He was the source of that musk, she decided, although it was no stronger here than it had been outside.

"So. Grace."

He seemed to be tasting her name, rather than asking it. The woman in brown must have told him, of course.

"No family name?"

She tilted her head, studying him. "Would it make a difference if I did?" Her family was all back east, so far as to not even exist—or perhaps it was she who no longer existed, for them. The living weights they had put on her seemed less binding, here, either way. No more the daughter of John Cooper Olcott, no longer the despair of Patience Olcott...

His hair wasn't chestnut, she realized, but black. Or perhaps that was merely the change of light. His eyes were a deep golden brown, set deep under a high brow, and...

She shook herself. Was this even the same man he'd seen, out front? She firmed her lips, and studied him more carefully. Yes, it was the same man, though her first glance at him did not hold up so well at close range: he was definitely older, hair darker and skin paler, but she was convinced that it was him.

"You are a surprise," he said, more to himself than her. "The winds will have their amusement, I suppose."

"Excuse me," she said, aware that her tone was less polite than her words. "But who are you?"

Those golden-brown eyes widened, and this close she thought they almost brightened, before he leaned back in his chair and started to laugh.

She waited, only practice in being mocked allowing her to keep her shoulders straight and her fingers loose on her lap.

"You truly have no idea where you are, do you." This seemed to—not so much amuse as delight him, she decided.

"A town called Flood, in an unnamed saloon, locked in a room with a madman."

"You are not entirely wrong," he said, but his voice was soft, and yes, definitely ... amused. She should be angry, or at least worried, if this man held as much power as others seemed to deed him, but instead felt a tingle of something else, something that had her meeting that gaze squarely, waiting, rather than attempting to flee.

Whatever happened here, at least it was better than what she had left. It had to be.

"You have, however, heard of me, if not by name," the man went on. "Beyond the Territory, in the so-called civilized lands, they call me the Devil."

There was silence in the small room, an almost palpable pressure against her ears, and then she thought she could hear her own heartbeat, slow as a metronome, before sound came rushing back as she let out a gasp of laughter.

If you're not careful, the devil will take you, girl. How many times had she heard that, as a child? Even time she showed anger, or dared contradict an elder, as though these were sins akin to those of Cain.

She shook off the memory and lifted her chin, refusing to let him see the tremor that had passed through her at his words. Those dour men had pressed their Bibles when they lectured her, dreaming of hellfire and damnation sweeping her off, not ... this.

Of course she knew of the Devil, the so-called Master of the Territory. You sold your soul to him when you crossed the river, the stories said. Or, other stories claimed, you only sold your soul when you settled down; if you kept moving, he couldn't catch you. Or, other stories said...

There were many stories and very few of them agreed, save that the Devil was the sole power in the Territories, and God Himself had given up on those lands, or perhaps never found them to begin with.

Her mother, rest her soul, had scoffed at that. "The devil does not take human form, Grace," she'd told her daughter, one smooth hand resting on her own Bible, the gilt lettering of the cover faded from endless reverent handling. "He has no need; we do too much of his work for him."

She might go to the devil some day, but she did not think today was that day. Besides, what he had said...

"They call you the Devil," she repeated carefully. "You do not claim that title for yourself?"

"A title that is self-claimed is meaningless." He leaned back in his chair, and reached for a slender cigar that had been waiting on his desk. He did not cut or light it, merely rolled it between his fingers, studying it for a moment, rather than her. "Something given unasked? That has meaning. And power."

Abruptly, that gaze returned to her face. "Why did you come to Flood?"

It was less a question than a demand for a response, and she bit back her automatic reaction, to refuse an answer from sheer willfulness. This was not one of those dour men; if he was the Master of the Territory, he had every right to ask her, and expect a response.

She could give him a handful of answers, each one as true as the other. Whim, or chance, or fate, or sheer cussedness, or the desire to go as far from other people as she could.

"The winds pushed me here," she said, instead, remembering the way the wind had seemed to wrap itself around her skirts, drawing her attention to the lesser path.

"Yes. That much we gathered."

Had they? There was something in his words, something in what they were saying—and weren't—that intrigued her. "The bartender, Iktan? He said I smelled of the wind."

"He's rarely wrong in these matters. In fact, I'm not sure I remember the last time he was. It would be annoying, if it weren't so useful." The man—the Devil—put the cigar back down on the desk, and steepled his fingers in front of his mouth, studying her over the tips. A shock of blond hair fell over his forehead and she had the odd urge to push it back.

"The winds are none of mine to control nor call," he went on. "They have their own mysteries, and act on their own whims. But I find it useful to take their counsel, when they choose to give it."

She licked her lips, suddenly aware that they'd gone dry. "You speak as though the wind is ... alive."

He smiled, and she wished he hadn't.

"The winds—there are many of them, each with their own ... mood, you may call it. And I do not claim to call them alive, but they are certainly aware."

She thought again of how the wind had belled her skirts and pushed at her knees. She thought of the voice she'd thought she'd heard, that faint echo of laughter. She had thought it ... she had thought it her imagination, or at most a hint, her brain's impulse. The idea that something might be *directing* her....

Uncanny, she thought again, and then a familiar, if unwelcome, flare of anger warmed her spine. "And it—they—sent me here?" She might travel to the ends of civilization, it seemed, and *still* she would be shaped to someone else's—some*thing* else's whim.

He rolled the cigar slowly against the desk, the leaf crackling slightly under his touch. "I doubt anything so overt, although I am open to surprise. More ... they may have noted you in passing, and thought it amusing to direct you into my path. Or, perhaps, me into yours. You dislike that idea."

Her expression must have let slip her distaste. "I dislike anything attempting to manipulate me,"

"Yes, I imagine you do," he said, his own expression turning thoughtful. "I imagine you prefer to be the one doing the manipulating."

He did not sound disapproving. "A woman's lot in life is to manipulate those around her. It is the only way we may gain even the smallest of control over our own lives."

His lips twitched, then regained their composed line. "Your mother must have been a formidable woman," he said. "Or your grandmother, perhaps?"

"My mother." There was a faint pang at the thought. "She died two winters past."

"And you miss her."

"I ... no." The admission slipped out, past lips usually far more guarded.

"No. You loved her, but you do not miss her. You believe she'd gone to a better place?"

A faint shrug, two years of ache, and an odd sense of freedom impossible to explain. Unnatural child, her aunt had called her, more than once. "She is gone."

There was an absence where she had been, a space that had once been filled, but even in the first days after, she had felt only that absence, not the raw grief that had been expected of her.

Odd and unnatural, her father had called her.

"And, freed of that tether, you left your home, left all you belonged to, and came ... here."

Suddenly he smiled, not the faint twitch of earlier, nor the closed-mouthed smirk she'd disliked, but an open, almost joyful shift. "Of course you did."

E ven as it happened, she could not quite follow the movement that took her from the Devil's study to a small room on the upper floor of the saloon, her bag placed on top of the low wooden drawers, her few items of clothing hung in the wardrobe, even her stockings folded and placed in the drawers, her brush and comb next to the now-empty bag. There was a basin and a pitcher of water on a stand by the narrow window, and an oil lamp hanging from a hook in the ceiling, a metal hook-and-cup hung on the wall for lighting or dousing it.

"Your room," the woman in brown had said, pushing open the door. "Mostly our girls share, but you're too old for that nonsense. Peace and quiet's what you need."

"Evening meals starts at seven in the evening," the girl who'd been putting away her things was chattering now, fussily adjusting the wardrobe, as though there were twice as many clothes in there. Somehow, she thought there might be, as though each chemise and skirt had multiplied as they were shaken out and put away. "We don't hold on ceremony, but that's when the food's first ready. Just come down and have what you want. Cook starts coffee when he wakes up, so whenever you come down it'll be ready, there's nobody who wakes before him, not even the boss."

"What's your name?" She'd been told, she thought, but there was nothing but a grey haze in her thoughts, where it should be.

"Bets. It's short for Elizabeth but the boss said I was too wee a thing to need such a long name, and it stuck even when I got bigger. I've been here since I was seven."

"You're a servant?" The hired girls back home had chattered endlessly, but only to each other. Still, she supposed her own status was ... uncertain, here. She wasn't even sure, herself, what she'd agreed to.

"Indentured til I'm sixteen. That's next year. I'm going to get married then. Boss said we had to wait, so Aaron's been working his daddy's farm, earning land of his own."

The girl turned, and clasped two fingers over her

mouth. "And here I am chatting when you're likely wore out and just want to rest. I'll be out of your way in a twitch, let me just fetch you a towel for your basin. The sheets are fresh, but if the pillow's not to your liking, just let me know. I run the linens, so I know where everything is."

If she hadn't been tired before, the girl's activity would have made her so. Grace managed a smile and a thank you, and waited until the girl had slipped out the door before she sat down on the bed, staring around her.

She was part of the Devil's household now, it seemed. If only she knew what that *meant*.

"Grace. Grace! You're mist-dreaming again."

"Was I? I'm sorry." She looked down at the work in her hands, gratified to note that she hadn't dropped the dish into the sink and broken something, this time. Mist-dreaming. That was a new term, among the many new words she'd learned in the past weeks. She supposed it was as descriptive as any.

"It's a nice change from Bets always talking," Anna said, shrugging. "You're different." Anna frowned, glancing sideways over the sink. "I don't mean that in a bad way. Not exactly."

"I'm not offended." She wasn't. She couldn't be, not when it was the truth.

She finished wiping down the dish Anna had given her, and placed it with the others, then waited for the girl to finish with the one she was washing. It should have been lowering to be assigned kitchen duties with this child, as though she were still a girl herself, but the other option would be to serve drinks among the players, and neither she nor the boss had thought that was a good idea.

Not yet, anyway, he had said, that cigar in his hand again, rolling it between long fingers like a mountebank might move a coin.

Not ever, she had wanted to retort, but caution and training held her tongue. She was not the sort to let loose among others. She had none of the virtues of service, no smooth tongue nor gentle nature. He had seen that, he must have, and yet...

And yet, weeks later, she still had no idea of what he wanted from her. All this ... the boss had been all that was generous, but she did not pretend that it would not have a cost, eventually, and for more than her work as a household maid might bring.

Particularly a maid they did not need.

There were eleven souls living in the saloon proper: Iktan, the bartender, and the cook, a lean, pale specter of a man named Louis, were the only men. The boy she'd seen before, Moses, lived with his father, the farrier, outside of town proper. Judit was the woman in the brown dress; she ran the saloon for the boss, and all those within it: Anna and Bets, and a slip of a child unfairly named Prudence, who couldn't be more than seven, but ran messages and generally got underfoot like an unruly cat, plus Zinnia and Edward, who dealt at the tables, and Maggie, who served drinks, and possibly offered more. She didn't ask, and didn't judge. The boss.

And her now, of course.

"It's not a bad difference," Anna went on, suddenly realizing she was still holding a soapy dish, and dunking it to rinse before handing it over for drying. "And it's not because you're from away; Maggie and Judit and Zinnia are all from away too, although Judit's been here so long I don't know if she even counts any more, plus she's Judit. You're different the way Winter is different."

Winter was Native, the first—and so far only—one Grace had met, yet. If they were all similar to Winter—quiet, observant, seldom smiling as she delivered the laundry and took away the soiled sheets—she thought she could do worse to be different like that.

"We are both far from home," she said, the rhythm of handing off plates shifting to the more delicate washing of glassware. "Perhaps that is it."

Winter's people had all died when she was a young girl. She lived in a cottage outside town, with a small red dog who waited by the door when she came in.

There were tribes nearby, but Grace had been told they generally left Flood be. The Agreement that bound all settlers did not constrain them in the same way, and the boss had little authority over them. It seemed an odd way to rule, but the boss had only laughed and denied ruling anything, not even the saloon.

"I think it's the way you look at us. As though..." Anna ran out of words. "I don't know," she said with a shrug. "You're just different. It's interesting."

Back home, different had gotten her pitying looks and cold shoulders. Here, she was 'interesting.' That alone was worth having to wash dishes and fold laundry.

At least she didn't have to sweep.

"I'm not—"

A shout from the main room made them both freeze. It was loud, male, and angry. Grace had not heard a voice raised anger since she came here; even the overly-affectionate would-be gambler who'd been fool enough to touch Bets hadn't gotten more than a firm suggestion from the boss that he remove himself immediately. The boss didn't need to raise his voice to get results, and folk knew better than to raise theirs when he was around.

But the boss wasn't there tonight. He'd gone off somewhere that morning, without explanation, and the business of the saloon had continued without him, the players who'd come to test themselves against him patiently accepting the news that they'd have to wait.

Another shout, and a woman's voice—Judit, speaking sternly but not loudly. Then came the sound of something heavy being shoved across the planked floor, and Grace was at the kitchen door before she realized it, cotton dish towel tossed over one shoulder, an old apron tied around her waist.

Foolish, a voice whispered, a familiar scold. *Go back where it's safe, go back where you will not be noticed.*

But something drew her, her mind clearing of the earlier mist, sharp and bright as icicles dripping from a roof.

She became aware of Anna at her back, a warm, frightened weight she did not have time for, and elbowed her away as gently as she could before returning her attention to the scene in front of her.

Two chairs had been overturned, the game table shoved back—that had been the noise they'd heard. Judit stood between two men, her hand on one chest, the other hand up as though to warn someone away.

The other man did not look inclined to be warned, least of all by a woman more than a head shorter than he.

"What's this, then?" Grace asked, taking a further step into the room, feeling that sharpness crackle in her head like winter ice, an almost-forgotten pleasure.

"Grace, no." Judit's voice was barely a whisper, for all its intensity, and she ignored it.

She was only a scant hand taller than the other woman, but she was broader in the shoulder, and she used that to put herself into the picture. "What's this then," she asked again, ignoring Judit and the man behind her, directing her attention to the other man. She could hear that flat tone in her voice her mother had despaired of, the one that made people blink and look away from her, but this man met her gaze without hesitation, staring down not as though to ask how dare a woman challenge him, but with the look of someone ready to start a fight no matter what.

She stared back, and waited.

"That ... demon-lover cheated me."

"I did no such thing." The man behind Judit was indignant, but his voice quivered in fear. Of the man threatening him? Of the accusation? The insult? She had no way to tell, and truthfully did not care.

"I saw no sign of cheating," Judit said, voice certain, and in a normal day, that would have been enough to restore calm. You did not challenge Judit any more than you challenged the Devil; in this place and instance, they were effectively the same: she spoke with his authority. But the look in the man's eyes, the set of his shoulders, told Grace that he would not back down. It was entirely possible he could not, but more than that, he did not wish to.

She knew that look. He wanted to hurt something. The claim of cheating was only giving him excuse.

Back across the River, back in civilization, placing herself in front of him might have been enough to shame him. Might: there were men there who took pleasure in damaging things weaker than they, though mostly they did it out of sight. But the Territory, she had learned already, was different.

She approved. Not that men could be brutes in

public, but that there was no pretense that they were not brutes.

"You wanted an excuse," she told him, her voice pitched low to carry only between the two of them. "The itch under your skin got too bright, the worm in your brain too hungry. Did you come here looking for it, I wonder, or did it burst out when your cards turned wrong?"

He snarled, but his attention was on her now, not the man behind her. Better.

"Would you dared to have entered the saloon if you knew the Devil were at home, or did you lurk outside until you saw him ride out, aware he'd have torn you to shreds if you came in here like that?"

She knew no such thing, but suspected it: the boss kept an easy hand on the reins but no-one doubted for an instant that they were his hands, at all times. For all that he demurred mastery, Flood was his, and all things that occurred within it were his as well.

But the devil was not here, and she was.

His face hardened, the only warning, and she ducked under the arm that swung at her, tucking her skirt against her knees so there was nothing to trip her, feeling the push of the winds against her legs, though there was no breeze that could find its way past walls and doors.

She did not know how to fight, had never learned to punch or grab, but she knew how to slap, and how sharply she could kick. Men braced for a blow to the body, the stomach or the face. They never protected against the shin, or the back of their knee.

He hit the floor, but she did not think he would stay there, not for long. She danced back, finger curling into her palm with the need to strike, to take him down so that he would stay down, but her breathing stayed steady, her eyes clear and her ears catching the scrape and scuffle of Iktan coming over the bar, a length of rope in his hands.

"Well done," he said, even as he looped the rope over the man's wrists, stringing the rope up between his shoulders and looping it around the man's neck, making a self-fulfilling noose, if he tried to struggle or get free. She nodded, letting her fingers ease, forcing the hot fury, the need to *break* something, back down.

It took too long; she'd been careless, not vigilant enough. And now would the inevitable aftermath. For all the bartender's brusque approval, now she would look up and see the others back away from her, eyes cautious, faces if nor disproving, then dubious, doubtful. Different would become dangerous, not interesting.

"Tie him the rail outside," Judit said, her voice cool. "Let him simmer in the dust for a while, and consider his flaws while we wait for the boss to return."

It was the sort of thing Grace might have suggested, if she'd thought of it. There was a reason she and Judit got along without too much scraping, she supposed.

"You can't—" the man's voice cut off in a choke: Iktan had tugged the rope harder than was perhaps needful, as he escorted him to the door.

"All right, everyone," Judit said, her voice cool and controlled. "Grace, breathe. The rest of you, back to whatever you were doing before this minor contretemps, and don't think I didn't see where you laid your cards, Johnny!"

Johnny, a slight-built rancher who came in every seven-day to lose his paycheck on rotgut and poker, grinned without shame. He'd sleight of hand that would astonish a professional cheat, but he never used them at the table for real stakes, only to amuse.

It took all kinds to fill the devil's tables, she supposed.

Judit gave Grace a calculating look, and she braced herself for recriminations or scolding, but the woman merely shook her head, lifted her eyes to the ceiling, and went back to the table where she had been dealing cards, picking up the deck and calling for a reshuffle, the pot would stand.

And like that, it was over. As though violence had never existed within these walls, as though she had not, however briefly, shed the polite skin she draped over herself, as though...

"Grace?"

She shook herself, feeling the fragments of circles breaking off in shards, her mind softening again. "Yes."

"That was foolish of you." Zinnia could move like a fetch when she had a mind to, the only sound the soft whisper of her skirts. She wore slippers instead of sensible shoes, and her hair was bound under a darkly-patterned scarf that emphasized the broad planes of her cheekbones, skin so brown even lamplight seemed lost in it.

"I'm never foolish." It wasn't a brag, simply the honest truth. She had seen the situation, considered what could be done, and done it because she could.

And, she admitted, because she had wanted to. Because it had felt good.

"You're a strange one, Grace. Strange even for this town. Weren't you frightened?"

"No."

She never had been, that she could recall. Uncertainty, yes, she knew that, and she had learned caution, but never fear. She supposed she lacked the imagination for it, or whatever it was that fed other people. It was only one of the things she'd been found lacking in, and not one that had ever seemed a terrible loss.

But it made her strange. It made others uncomfortable.

Zinnia eyed her, and she lifted her chin and stared back, daring the other woman to say something else.

"Well, if we can't teach you to be cautious, we'll need to teach you to use that knife."

That … she had not been expecting.

Mornings were generally quiet in Flood. The younger girls woke early, as did the cook, and Grace would come to awareness, her face half turned into her pillow, and hear them rattling about below stairs, but it was a comforting noise, not one that roused her to wakefulness. Even with the window closed, the smell from the blacksmith's forge crept in, mixing with the bitter coffee and yeasted bread smells rising from the kitchen, wound under and around the thread of spices and cigar leaf that lingered even in rooms the devil never entered. All is well, the combination told her. All is under control.

Still, a part of her was alert, always, pushing against that weight of silence. She should be doing something, being somewhere, anticipating the next thing that would be required of her, finding a way to mold herself into its demands.

But there was nothing she needed to do, just then. Her bowels were calm, and the mattress cool and comfortable enough that it was pleasurable to simply rest there, eyes closed, breathing soft, and wait. That faint movement below, and a distant clang and rattle from outside on the street, yes, but the upper floor of the saloon was heavy and still.

Not a wonder, that everyone yet slept; the last player had shuffled off, somewhat worse for drink, long after the chiming clock in the foyer had struck eleven. The younger girls had long gone to sleep, Iktan and Louis gone who-knew-where, but the rest of them had stayed up well past that, barefoot and hair loose, sharing out the last of a bottle of bitter gin while Judit showed off her dealing, the swish and thwack of cards fanning from out of her hands the sound that eventually, one by one, carried them off to sleep.

She should doze back to sleep, Grace knew. Eventually, however, restlessness drove her to throw back the coverlet and swing her legs over, shivering slightly when bare feet met cool wooden floor. Her toes scrunched, then straightened, and she reached for the napped cotton wrapper thrown over the back of the chair, tying it securely around her waist before moving to the washbasin, and pouring water from the pitcher to splash on her face.

It would be a long day ahead. The saloon itself did not open until midday, but after breakfast she would be expected to meet Zinnia and Maggie for her first lesson with a knife. She did not like the thought of it, uneasy with the weight of it, even imagined, in her hand, but hadn't been able to explain to the other woman why she thought it a dangerous plan.

The sky outside her window, what little she could see of it, was thick with clouds. Bets would know if it was going to rain, she had a sense for such things. Appropriate, for a soon-to-be farmer's wife.

"All I have is a sense for violence," she told the faint reflection in the window. She hadn't realized it bothered her. Or, rather, that it bothered her that it did not bother

her. Not until the day before, not until she'd been invited to *train* that sense, rather than control it.

It seemed an invitation to disaster, but she did not know how to explain that to them. Not without laying open what she was, and that—she could not do that. Could not risk even this fragile place she'd found, where they looked at her and did not flinch from what they found.

If only she knew how to do the same.

Grace dried her face with the towel hung by the side of the basin, and shed her night rail for a simple dark brown dress, lacing the waist comfortably and tucking her feet into a pair of deerhide slippers before opening the door to the hallway. Putting her hands to work often made her thoughts still. Louis always had use for another pair of hands.

One other door in the hallway was ajar, the others tight-closed. The aroma of fresh bread was stronger than brimstone, here, and the clatter of metal and plates told her breakfast was likely ready for the earliest risers. But she was not hungry, and something more than coffee, or the desire to be distracted drove her down the stair, slippersoft footfalls on polished wooden steps, her fingers light on the rail.

The scent of brimstone and musk intensified.

The office door was open, as though he had been waiting for her. Of course he had, she thought, even as she once again took the chair opposite his desk, composing her skirt carefully and clasping her hands on her lap with a pose of studied attention.

He must have returned in the small hours of the morning, likely not gone to bed yet, assuming he even slept. Four days gone; wherever he'd been, it had worn on him. He looked tired, she thought, before the lines of his face smoothed, for an instant making him seem younger than she.

"Stop that," she snapped, and he grinned, teeth showing in that disconcerting smile of his before composing himself into more civilized lines.

"I hear you're to begin lessons today."

She did not ask how he knew that. He simply knew things, if he chose to.

"I suppose I am."

He hrmmmmed under his breath. "Did you enjoy yourself?"

She frowned at him. "No." No need to ask what he was talking about. Only one thing of note had occurred while he was gone.

"No? It simply needed to be done and you did it?"

She lifted her chin, almost in surprise, and frowned back at him, her eyes narrowing. "It's ... not that simple."

"Of course it is."

"Of course it isn't!"

She suspected that no-one else spoke to him like this, or she thought they didn't, anyway. Judit might say whatever she wished, in private, but in public she deferred to him, and the others.... He was the boss. The wouldn't think of defying him, even if they disagreed, and she'd yet to see any sign that they knew how to do that.

"Judit would have handled it," he said, and tucked the cigar under one finger, then another, before rolling it in his palm the way another might pet a cat. The smell of fresh tobacco, green and earthy, made her nostrils tickle.

"Is she upset with me?"

"If she were, you would be in no doubt about it."

That was true, and one of the reasons she remained

in the saloon: Judit left no room for uncertainty in how she felt. Except, of course, where she gave no hint at all, but those were matters beyond Grace's ken or caring.

She waited, watching those golden eyes watching her. They could do this all day; she felt no need to blink or look away.

"Why did you step between them, if not for enjoyment, and not because it needed to be done?"

She drew a breath deep through her nose, and exhaled through her mouth, a familiar, calming motion, although she was neither upset nor startled by the question. Perplexed, perhaps.

"They would have come to blows, despite Judit's efforts. He *wanted* to come to blows."

"And you...." His gaze flickered, something deep in his eyes rising for a moment. "Ah."

She waited, but he said nothing more. After a while, the thread-pull that had drawn her to his office dropped. She waited a moment, simply to say that she came and went of her own accord, then decided it was time for breakfast, after all.

She left the door open behind her, a defiant rudeness, and heard his soft chuckle follow her into the kitchen.

Bets had just slid the morning's breads out of the oven, slipping them onto the battered wooden worktable to cool, when Grace entered the kitchen. The girl looked up in surprise, and then lifted her arm so that her elbow pointed to where a coffee pot sat on the hob. "You look like you've a need for it," the girl said. "I heard you go into the office."

No questions: Bets was clearly curious, and gossip was as common here as anywhere else, but for all that the girl was a chatterbox, she never demanded the same of others. It was why Grace could stand to be around the girl, that respect for silence.

Bets had been a gift, in the earlier days: you learned useful things when other people chattered, and even if they weren't useful then, they might be later. But right then, Grace had a puzzle on her mind, and the girl might be useful in another way.

"He wanted to talk about the fight," Grace said, pouring herself a cup and letting the aroma fill her nostrils, overriding the scent of tobacco and brimstone, although nothing could ever truly drive it out. "Why I did it."

Bets shook her head, the pinned loop of her braid swinging almost violently. "Judit let him off too easy," she said. "Leaving a man outside over night to face the shame of others in the morning only works if the man has some to begin with, and we all know now he has none."

He'd been just as bullheaded in the morning, hung-over and ache-ridden, as he'd been the night before. She didn't know why Bets thought a night tied to a post would sweeten anyone's behavior. You were what you were. Then again, there were things that happened here that still confounded her understanding. Not the least of which was why no-one seemed to see her differently, after she'd shown what she could be. Were they all blind? Or did they ... simply not care?

"You." Louis was pointing at her, two thick fingers outstretched accusingly "Stop standing there wasting the girl's time. Come help me."

The boss might be unquestioned, and Judit unchallenged, but the cook was obeyed, no matter what task he handed you; if you did not know how to do it, you learned. And so she found herself learning how to gut and prepare rabbits for roasting.

No knowledge was ever wasted, her father had said more than once, and she supposed if she were ever to take the road again, rabbit would be a useful thing to prepare. But the feel of slick skin under her finders, the vibration of the paring knife along bone, made her hope she'd never have cause to do so.

However, when she was done, apron discarded and hands washed thoroughly with brown soap to remove the bloody bits, Bets seemed to have forgotten their previous conversation. She allowed herself to forget it, as well.

At least until Zinnia came to collect her for her first lesson.

"I do believe you're a natural at this," Maggie said, panting slightly.

She wiped her forehead with the cloth Zinnia gave her, and handed it back to the other woman, the wooden-bladed knife a too-warm weight in her hand. Her skirt was covered in dust, her skin still dotted with sweat, her hair likely as messy in its braid as Maggie's, and her legs were wobbling with exhaustion, although so far, all they had done was circle each other, with Maggie occasionally stepping forward to tap her on the arm or leg before retreating, then encouraging Grace to do the same.

So far, she hadn't managed to touch Maggie once. "Naturally poor, perhaps?"

They'd taken over the bare patch of ground at the far end of town that she now could tell was bare because it was used for practices like this. Thankfully, there few who'd paused to watch were swiftly sent on their way by Zinnia's hard stare.

"Not," Maggie disagreed. "You aren't landing a blow, but you're not swinging wildly, either, or trying to do anything foolish. It took me almost a month of steady practice to learn not to do that."

"Grace has a very quiet mind," Zinnia said from her perch on the end of an upturned barrel. "Unlike you."

"There is nothing about me that is quiet," Maggie said, almost proudly, and lunched forward, her hand flicking up almost faster than she could follow.

Her eye, that was. Grace's arm moved without thought, the crack of the wooden blades against each other echoing off the buildings like thunder, and she ducked underneath and put her shoulder to Maggie's chest, shoving up at the taller woman until she felt a wobble, then shoving harder, until they both fell to the ground, Grace on top, both blades clattering out of their hands and onto the packed dirt.

There was a moment of stunned silence, and then Zinnia's slow clap. Maggie rolled her eyes, shoving Grace off her. "That would have been well-done, if you'd actually held onto your blade. Now up, let's try again."

A week passed, and then a month. The days grew longer, and the hills outside of town turned green and blue with flowers, and then golden with crops, until a half-year had passed, and memory of life before Flood began to haze.

She became reasonably proficient with her knife, although Maggie warned her that holding back in a true fight would likely get her killed. Judit taught her how to deal faro, and she covered a table some nights, although she still had no true skill for it. The boss occasionally asked her opinion of things occurring across the River, and kept her informed of events, including an uprising of natives laying siege to military forts back east. She had spent that night sitting on the porch, watching the stars slip overhead, and wondered if such a thing might happen here.

To all appearances, she had settled well into life in Flood. And yet, Flood did not sit well on her bones. She *wanted* it to. If the Territory was not perfect, it was far better than what she had left behind. If some folk were cautious around her, others seemed to find her oddness as ordinary as every day. But fear of another incident kept her tense, and not even the joy of learning how to fight properly, to do only the damage she intended, could ease the worry of stepping wrongly again, of crossing a line that even Flood could not accept.

She was not afraid. She had never been afraid. But she worried.

G race began taking longer walks, out past the buildings that comprised Flood proper, following the curve of the river, watching horse and farmer drag a battered scythe between rows, slighter forms following to gather the grains. She did not know their names, these folk who lingered on the edges of Flood. They were nothing to her, and she nothing to them.

"There are too many people in this world to care about."

She had never seen the boss outside of the saloon. She had not even been certain he could pass the doors, though obviously, of course, he could and did.

"Aren't we supposed to care about everyone?"

The boss shrugged, nonchalant. He leaned as though there was a tree at his back, certain that the air would hold him, and studied the farmhands as they worked, unaware of being observed. "There's supposed to, and then there's able to. You can't hold every grain of sand in your hand, and only a fool tries."

"And there are no fools in the Territory."

"Not for long, anyway. Not alive."

"And what of the fool who cannot care for anyone?"

"All we need is one."

"One person?"

He made a thoughtful, dismissive face, skin shading pale and then ruddy, as though to reflect something within. "One thing."

That night, at Edward's table, she noted two guests playing well but not brilliantly, the pile of coins at their knuckles never rising nor falling particularly. She wasn't certain what had drawn her attention, perhaps the way they sat, or how they did not speak to each other, but occasionally leaned in as though sharing something in silence while the other players maintained the easy flow of chatter she'd learned was common with regulars.

Watch the players as much as the cards, Judit had told her, watching her flip the cards, fingers still fumble-thick but learning. Anything that seems odd, or unusual, or out of place. Your instincts will know before you do; trust them.

So she watched. Close, but not a couple. Siblings, mayhap, or cousins. Raised together. They held the pasteboard cards in easy fingers, their mouths and eyes set in relaxed lines that said nothing, gave nothing away. They drank, but slowly, and shook their heads with a smile when Zinnia offered to freshen their glass. Too many players imbibed too easily, Judit had said, and so lost hands they otherwise should have won.

But still, there was nothing about them that warranted further exploration, and she might have put them out of her head as unusual but not particularly noteworthy, had the devil not chosen that night to take his table.

He did not, always. Most nights, the center table remained untouched, the players circulating other tables, giving the empty chairs wide berth as though to brush against one would be to give offense. Even those who worked there were careful, skirting the edges with experienced curves of hip and arms.

Some nights, the boss was a brightly visible presence, moving through the room like a ripple in a lake, pausing to speak to some, ignoring others. Or he might be nowhere to be seen until well past closing, or not be seen at all. There was no pattern she could determine, no schedule or clue as to what he might do.

She half-suspected he did not know himself, until he was doing it.

But some nights he pulled out the dealer's chair and seated himself, long fingers sliding open a fresh deck of playing cards and fanning them with expert skill, the flickerthwack of cards hitting the green felt surface somehow louder, stronger, than the sound from any other table.

Not every seat at his table filled, even when every other chair in the room was taken. Often, only one or two players pulled out chairs to join him. Occasionally, there would be only one, and those nights Judit served the drinks herself, her hand often resting gently on the player's shoulder, either in encouragement or sympathy.

Grace had seen that happen only a handful of times, but she did not know what it meant.

The winding clock against the wall had only just marked ten o'clock when he took his seat, just as the game at the other table was coming to a close. She had been helping behind the bar, polishing glassware while Iktan poured, the two of them creating an easy dance that allowed her time to watch and learn, as well.

The older of the pair had folded, watching while the younger won the small pot. They cashed out of the game with good grace, sliding a quarter-coin across the felt to Edward, and carried their remaining silver to the devil's table.

He greeted them with a nod, as though he'd been waiting for nothing save their arrival, the cards face down in front of them even as they pushed a coin each onto the felt.

Judit leaned an elbow on the polished wood of the bar and Iktan placed two glasses on her tray without being asked. Grace knew enough by now to note that it was better quality whiskey than he usually served; the golden amber color was what the boss himself drank, the few times she saw him indulge.

She watched Judit move across the room, saw how the two players did not react when Judit placed the glasses by their elbows, but the boss looked up and gave her a nod of thanks.

Grace did not know what that meant, either.

Maggie saw her watching, as she handed over her tray of empty glasses to be washed and dried. "They're not here to prove anything," she said. "You can always tell."

"Tell what?"

"When they need a bargain," Maggie said, her kohl-smudged eyes widening as though to emphasize her words. "What else?"

"Of course," she said, and that seemed to satisfy the other woman.

She had known that, yes. It had been explained to her that first day: You came to Flood if you needed something from the devil. And the devil ... made deals. That was what they said in more civilized lands. You sold your soul to survive in the devil's lands.

Except she'd seen nothing of that, herself. Everyone needed something, of course. She had needed a place to be, an occupation for her hands, and he had offered it, but there had been no bargain, no deal. Her soul, as far as she knew she had one, remained her own. Didn't it?

Had she made a bargain without knowing it? It seemed unlikely; surely such an agreement could not hold, not in courts of man or god. But then, there were no barristers here to argue the point, and the only judge she'd even heard of was a man who came riding through on occasion—such occasions often years-between. Judit had muttered once about finding a judge and sticking him to place with a nail, if need be, but if the devil ruled the town, what need had they of a judge?

It was confusing, and she did not like confusion.

"It's my break, can you—?"

She took the tray Zinnia handed her, watching the other woman slide smoothly out the door, the fading sunlight red in the open outline before the door closed again. There were no windows in the saloon proper, no way to tell time was passing save for the occasional chime of the winding clock that spoke only when it was time to close. She had not realized that, before.

She refilled glasses and loaded the empties without a wobble, the particular tilt and bend now familiar to her,

her gaze resting on the players' faces rather than their cards, her smile pleasant yet promising nothing. While some looked up to say thank you, most barely acknowledged her, save a distracted nod of thanks. She did not mind; unlike some of the other girls, she had no interest in furthering an acquaintance with them.

It was none of her business what other folk did, or where they came from. That was a thing she did understand about the Territory: idle gossip might be the devil's whisper elsewhere, but there was an understanding once you crossed the river, that a man's—or a woman's—business was their own. You asked nothing that was not offered first.

That suited her to her toes, that reticence. And yet she found herself still watching the two players as they passed cards across the green felt, wondering what interest they had for the devil, what had driven them to sit at his table.

What bargain did they seek to make, and how did the cards know?

And why did she even care?

They sipped from their glasses, and Judit refilled them, her fingers touching the back of their wrists gently, as the cards continued to turn. The hour grew later, the clock marking out the final hour, and the tables slowly emptied, players emptying glasses and collecting their winnings—or good-naturedly bemoaning their losses—before heading out, either to nearby farmsteads or the single boarding house where they slept four to a room for the joy of visiting Flood. The front door closed for the last time, and Maggie collapsed comfortably on the bench, the blue velvet of the cushions contrasting with her long blond hair as she let it down from its coronet, finger-combing it with a sigh of relief.

But still the devil dealt cards, the pile of silver bits on

his table rising and falling, but never disappearing entirely into either players' pocket.

"You're distracted tonight," Zinnia said, coming to stand behind her, breath uncomfortably warm on her shoulder. "Huh. They're good. He's better than she is, but they're both good."

"Better than the boss?"

Zinnia laughed. "He doesn't have to be good. He's dealing."

"He doesn't cheat?" She knew he didn't, knew he wouldn't, but something prodded her to ask nonetheless.

"He doesn't have to."

And finally, all that was left was the question that had been bothering her all evening, the question she'd never thought to ask, before. "What do they want from him?"

Zinnia shrugged. "Nobody knows. Nobody will know, 'cept him. That's how it works."

"But how do they ask—"

"They already have."

She frowned, watching the three of them at the table. There had been little conversation, asking for a new card or changing their bet, occasionally asking for water or a freshening of their glass. The boss didn't even seem to be watching them, their faces or their tells, only the cards as they were turned up and revealed.

Months of learning to deal, both faro and poker, but she still didn't understand the appeal of the games, or what pull it had over people. The cards were simply paper boards, the edges fancy-gilded, but nothing beyond the ordinary for all that, pips and markers in plain black ink on one side, a checkerboard pattern on the other. And each night there were new decks opened, the old ones burnt in case they'd been marked or spelled.

What could the cards be telling the boss, that he only watched them?

What were they playing for, that made that table so special?

She kept watching, even as the hour grew smaller. When the final game ended, the two players shook hands with the boss, solemn yet oddly joyful, and left with silver in their pocket and no sign of anything else about them different than when they'd come.

But something had changed in them. She knew it, although she had no understanding of how. They were different than they'd been when they came. And something in her needed to understand what, and why.

The chairs at the other tables were already tipped forward, the bar cleared, the glassware rinsed and ready for polishing. The rest had long ago slipped upstairs, heading for looser clothing and comfortable beds. Only she remained, sitting on the stairs, skirt tucked neatly under her knees, watching.

The boss looked up then, and she thought for certain he'd say something—explain, or perhaps scold her, or … something. But he merely pushed his chair back, finished the last sip of the glass he'd been nursing all night, and then was gone, and she had no better understanding of what she'd seen than before she'd known to look.

S he might have remained on that step all night and into the morning, save the hard wood under her backside turned cold, and she could not imagine explaining herself to Louis, or Judit, or whoever might find her at dawn, slumped like a child against the newel post.

She went through her evening ablutions slowly, folding her clothing into the wardrobe and slipping into her night rail, brushing out her hair and plaiting it for sleep, then crawling into her bed with the lamp turned down and the moonlight casting faint shadows against the curtains.

The pillow was firm, the sheets clean and soft, and her limbs were thick with exhaustion.

But sleep did not come. The saloon felt too still, too quiet, the oil from the lamp too heavy, the occasional distant yip and howl of night hunters too close, even though she knew full well they would not come into town, not when they had easier prey out in the fields.

"I could hear you thinking all the way down the hallway." Zinnia slipped into her room without invitation, closing the door gently behind her.

She shifted, so that her face was turned toward the door, squinting to make out the shape in the dim light. "I did not realize thoughts were so loud?"

"Yours are. Or maybe it's just that they're still new, so I hear 'em more."

"I apologize for keeping you from your sleep." Her tone might have been a bit sharp, but being told that she was *thinking* too loud? It seemed particularly unfair.

"I'll sleep in," the other woman said, coming to sit on the edge of the chair, her flannel wrap belted around her waist, thick curls bound up in a sash around her head. Even in the dim light, she could tell that the sash was a bright blue, the color of a butterfly's wing. "It's not like you to buzz so. Tell me."

She hadn't been aware of her own thoughts, so it was difficult at first to think of what to say, or even if she had anything to say at all.

"Have you ever asked the boss for anything?"

It was difficult to see Zinnia's expression, with only the moonlight, but the flash of teeth was unmistakable. "I have not, and pray I never need to. Not the way I'm thinking you mean."

"I don't know what I mean." It was only the shadows that allowed her to say that, to admit uncertainty, *vulnerability*. It made her wish to pull the coverlet to her chin, and pretend that the words had never come from her mouth, that she had been asleep from the moment Zinnia came into her room.

"The Territory does that to you," the other woman said. "Takes what you thought you knew and turns it downside-up, sometimes shakes it and breaks it entire, too. You've only been here, what, five months?"

"Six." Nearly eight, since she'd taken that first step onto the barge and crossed the river.

"Six. Seems a lifetime, doesn't it? I barely remember who I was, before."

She made a face at Zinnia's admission. "You were very young." According to Zinnia's stories, she'd barely been walking on her own when her parents came cross-river.

"Still am," and those teeth flashed again, a huffed laugh in the darkness. "But the Territory, it ages you up fast, even if it never really lets you get old, either. Not here, anyway. You stay in Flood, you'll see what I mean."

"And if I leave?" She hadn't thought about leaving, hadn't thought about anything much beyond day and day since she'd arrived, but now, in the darkness of the room, she wondered at that lack, that ... apathy. She'd always been a planner, from the time she was a child. But here, there was nothing to plan, nothing to arrange, or conceal. It simply ... was. And suddenly, it disturbed her.

"Are you thinking of leaving?" Zinnia sounded surprised. "Boss talks to you. He doesn't do that to many. You should stay, see what he's in mind for you."

"Because I want to, or because he wants to?" She felt something press inside, the mulish kick that always ended up making her father sigh.

"Probably both?" Zinnia's response disarmed her, unwillingly. "Let me ask you your own question. You ever ask the boss for anything?"

"No." Her thoughts earlier than evening returned to her like a stab. "Not even a job."

Something made Zinnia reach out, hard, warm fingers wrapping around her wrists like bracelets. "Not the boss who decides that, that's all Judit. She picks us like she's picking corn from a field, just 'this one and that one not that one nor that one,'" and her imitation of Judit's voice was uncannily perfect, making them both laugh, a little breathless.

"Tell me you never do that where she can hear," she said, slipping her hands from Zinnia's hold, drawing them back under the coverlet.

"Ah, she can hear everything, everywhere. There's no hiding from Judit. Not when you're in Flood, anyway. Did you know she put down the wardings? Back when the town wasn't even half the size it is now, she walked the line, trailing salt and sigils. And they sank right down through the dirt, burned themselves into the bone."

As a distraction, it was an effective one. "That's

impossible." She'd learned about wards since she crossed the river, same as you learned how to harness a mule or polish silver, as matter of course. They were what kept the haints and the demon from bothering the living, and warned bear and the like to stay clear. You painted them or carved them, or built them into walls, but nothing could put them into the ground, not like that.

"That's the story I was told. And I'm not going to say anything's impossible, not here. This is Flood, Grace."

There was weight in those three words that she didn't understand, still. Uncanny. Everything here was uncanny—save her.

She had wanted her entire life only to be ordinary, unexceptionable. To fit into the weave, not interrupt it. But she was starting to think, even here, it could not happen.

Zinnia was not easily distracted. "You asked about the boss—why? Because of those two who were here tonight? The ones at his table?"

She pulled the coverlet up over her shoulder, then shoved it away again, plumping the pillow under her head with more vigor than was required, suddenly feeling restless and petulant as a child. "Didn't my thoughts tell you?"

"I know you're noisy, dearling, not what the noise is."

"I can't stop..." not thinking about them, particularly, but why they had come. What they had wanted. And if they'd gotten it.

Zinnia waited.

"Bargains." The word felt odd, sounded odd, as though she'd said it too many times, even though she'd not spoken it out loud, before.

"They say ... well, they say things about him. About

everyone who lives here. That we all make a bargain with him. But ... most folk never even come to Flood." The family she'd traveled with had never mentioned the devil, never seemed to even know they were near his home, when they left her off. And while folk came into town, some of 'em on a regular basis ... she'd seen more people come and go through Landing than she'd seen in Flood, and she'd only been there a fortnight.

"No. Most don't. Some folk come to play the boss just 'cause they can. It's a thing they can puff about, later, say they faced off against the devil, and walked away with silver in their pockets. Some of 'em like the challenge—they come with their best cheats, and see if they can get away with anything."

"And they never do," she ventured, but Zinnia shook her head, the edges of her headscarf swaying.

"Some do. The boss is good but some cheat better. But they never get away with it twice, that's for certain. Thing is, some folk who do come don't want anything of the boss except to have been here. That's all most folk need: to have him here. Like ... like the natives do that thing, where they don't actually fight? They just steal something from another tribe, or cut someone's braid in a fight, or something that says "if I'd wanted to I could have but I didn't, and we both know it for the rest of our lives." That kind of thing. They know it only goes so far and no more, and the boss isn't going to get mad. Not at that."

She nodded as though she had any idea what Zinnia was speaking of. "But he's not safe." Only a fool would think the devil was safe.

"No. Oh, no. No more'n anything's safe, and you either learn that or you die a fool. But ... after the ones who don't need him, and the ones who only need small things ... If you need something, if you got a desire that burns you so hot you can't sleep for it, can't breathe for it, safe isn't what you're looking for. That's when people come to Flood to make a Bargain."

Nothing's safe. The other woman had been so casual about it, as though of course all things were dangerous. But what if they did not *want* to be?

She pulled herself upright, pushing the pillow against the headboard and curling her legs under the coverlet. "How does it happen?"

"What, bargaining? I don't know. Just that folk come filled with need, and they leave with it sated. The boss knows, and Judit, and they're the only ones who need to. We just... make sure they get to the table, if they need to be there." She heard Zinnia shift, start to say something and then exhale, as though uncertain she wanted to say anything at all. "You just curious, Grace? Or is there another reason you're asking? A reason your thoughts are such a loud jumble they're keeping you awake?"

Need wasn't the right word. She understood need: you needed water and food, and sleep and clothing. You needed room to move, to breathe. But these were things that could be acquired, bought or traded or taken. What she felt was more. Worse.

"No. Nothing like that. I was just curious."

"Count yourself lucky, then," Zinnia suggested. "And try to get some sleep. I'd like to do the same."

"Zinnia." Another question pushed its way into her thoughts, shaking itself like a wet dog coming out of a stream. "Are we friends?"

She'd never had a friend. She wasn't sure she knew how to be one. But if Zinnia said they were …

Zinnia was a dark shadow in the doorway, the glimmerlight from the hallway catching the hem of her nightfall and the tangle of her headscarf, nothing more.

"Not friends," she said. "Sisters, though. If you'd like. Sleep, Grace."

The rest of the week passed without incident, but she found herself more distracted, the occasional urge to throw her tray—glasses and all—across the saloon held back only by fierce effort that left her irritable and sharp-spoken, until even Zinnia left her be.

Occasionally, she felt the boss' gaze rest on her, but he said nothing.

Four days after Zinnia came to her room, she woke too early after another restless night, her body heavy with exhaustion, her thoughts scratchy, as though they'd been dragged along the creekside until coated in sand. The sound of the heavy boots on the porch below, low murmur of mens' voices and the heavy slap of packages being transferred to the kitchen told her that the butcher was making his weekly delivery, and she hoped, idly, that they'd run out of rabbits this time.

Her foot itched, and she pushed off the coverlet to scratch it, frowning as she considered her options. The sky was still dark, but she knew that chasing sleep further would be a fool's ride. Better to make a virtue of inevitability: waking early meant that she could wash her hair thoroughly rather than trying to rush her bath before someone hammered an impatient fist on the door.

Afterward, her hair in a damp coil at the back of her neck, she sat on her bed and considered the booklet on the small table by her bed, left by a rider a month before, and passed among the saloon's inhabitants in an echo of the subscription library her mother had belonged to. She felt no desire to pick the story up again, although she had begun it with great enthusiasm the week before. Her mouth felt dry, and her flesh twitched under her skin, the strange restlessness that had kept her from sleeping all week transferring itself to a more physical ailment.

Was she falling ill? That might explain much, perhaps.

Lacking any appealing option, she laced up her shoes and went down the stairs, thinking at the last she could find a cup of coffee, and maybe something productive to do. As it turned out, she was not the only one who could not sleep. The newest girl, Antonia, was huddled on the upholstered divan pushed against the far wall. She was bundled in a thick flannel wrap, deerskin slippers lined with fleece on her feet, her nose a pink button and her eyes red-rimmed from sneezing, even as her fingers wrapped around an earthenware mug filled with something that steamed tendrils into the morning air, a small bowl of eggs waiting to be cracked into it, Judit's surefire—if horrid-tasting—remedy for congestion.

The girl had only joined them the week before, from a farmsteading a few hours' ride out—had Tonia brought sickness into the saloon? She made a quick movement with her fingers, a subtle charm meant to keep away evil humors, and shook her head. "You look terrible."

"I appreciate your honestly," Antonia said, but her voice made it clear that she didn't appreciate it at all.

"If I'd told you that you look lovely, you'd roll your eyes at me," Grace said in response. "And if I didn't say anything at all, you'd think I was rude."

The girl made a face, but acknowledged the truth of those words. "Just ... stick with good morning?"

"It's a terrible morning and we're both awake far too early."

"I ... all right, there's no arguing with that." She sneezed again, and took a sip of the hot liquid, grimacing as she did so. "Cook swears this will cure me, but it may kill me, first."

Iktan, bringing in a crate of glassware from the kitchen, snorted at that. "If medicine was pleasing, we'd choose to be sick," he said, placing the crate on the bar and reaching for the cloth he used to keep them sparkling.

"Nobody would choose to be sick," Antonia said, and wiped her nose with the crook of her arm. "It's miserable."

Maggie came in from the kitchen, a mug in her own hands, but from the dark smell of it, she had coffee, not a tisane. Her eyes were heavy-lidded, and she merely nodded at them as she went past and up the stairs.

"Nobody slept well last night," Antonia noted. "My da used to say that meant there was a bad star over us."

She'd never heard that phrase before, and said so.

"Ah, it's a Ka'ayini saying. Da grew up running with them, picked up all sorts of language Ma didn't like him using, but some of it slipped through."

"Your father ... grew up with natives?"

Antonia nodded. "Their farmstead used the same stream to water the crops as the local tribe used, so they saw each other regular enough, seemed natural for the boys to play together, I guess. Oh, Grace, your *face*."

She had no idea what her face looked like, just then.

Antonia shook her head, smiling down into her mug. "I know you're new to the Territory, but whatever nonsense they filled your head with back where you were born, about the 'terrible savages' here, I'll wager not even a thimbleful was true."

She didn't bother to protest she'd been here long enough, nor that she'd never listened to the stories. Tall tales had held no interest for her, nor gossip, although she'd wondered a few times if she'd been more eager, or less, to cross the river, had she listened. She might have known more of the devil, too.

And likely much of that would have been wrong as well. Finding out for yourself was always better. She would have to judge the natives for herself as well, at some point, she supposed.

But they did not come to Flood. Of all the living souls in the Territory, they alone owed nothing to the devil.

The restlessness ached in her joints, took up residence in her bones, casting her exhaustion into high relief. She pressed her fingers into her elbows, as though to push it out, and returned to the earlier comment. "What does it mean, to have a bad star?"

"Oh … that there's something troublesome hanging above us, I suppose. Something big coming, or some change readying itself. It's all nonsense." But the girl didn't seem as certain as her words claimed.

"Nonsense," she repeated, thinking back to the feeling she'd had, the day she came to Flood. The voice she thought she'd heard, the push she'd definitely felt.

She'd smelled of the winds, Iktan had said. And the boss had said that Iktan was rarely wrong.

If anything brought troublesome change within the Territory, it was the winds. Only medicine men and would-be magicians dared stand within them, to gain the magic they carried, and the price the latter paid for what they learned was one she had no desire to pay.

She was odd, and perhaps uncanny, but she was not

mad. If the winds had sent her to Flood, it had been, as the boss had said, for their own entertainment, momentary and quickly forgotten. Whatever game they had played with her, she could only be glad it was over.

This bad star could have nothing do with her.

Antonia shrugged, taking another sip of her tisane. "If not foolishness, then mayhap just more we're not meant to understand. The whole of the Territory's its own self, isn't it? Half of it's hidden from us simply because of who we are, and likely all the more so for you, recent-come."

The girl's words caused something to shift in her chest. "What? Why?" Zinnia had said nothing of that, Judit hinted at nothing. The boss ... might have hinted at something of the sort, but the boss did things like that.

"Being born here ... I suppose it just comes more natural? There're things I couldn't explain to you, things I know just by knowing. Like wards. I know where they are when I come up on 'em, no matter who's laid them down. My ma couldn't, not all her life, and my da had to work at it. But my sisters and me, we all knew. Things like that. It's because we were born here."

Grace turned the example over, trying to stick other pieces into it. "Like the boss knowing what people want, just by them playing cards with him?"

"I suppose," Antonia said again. "He's been here the longest of any of us. Longer than the rocks, Ma says. Stands to reason he'd understand more."

The girl seemed to be done with that thought; she'd wondered and found a reasonable explanation and that was all she needed. She found herself envying the girl that certainty.

She hadn't been born here. She would never understand, never fit. But she hadn't fit where she'd *been* born to, either. Maybe they'd been right, back home: the problem was her, not wherever she was.

Maybe she had been made wrong, after all, and she would always feel this way.

"Good morning, ladies, Iktan."

Antonia jumped, still not accustomed to the way the boss could just show up out of nowhere. Her tisane spilled a little over her fingers, and the girl cursed, using the edge of her skirt to mop it up.

If no-one was sleeping well that night, he was not exempt. His shirtsleeves were rolled to his elbow, and the thatch of golden-brown hair was a tangled mess, as though he'd been running his fingers though it all morning, the same look she'd seen on her uncle's face, as though he'd been going over numbers all morning and they weren't making sense. But she'd never seen any indication that the boss knew what money the saloon took in, much less cared about making a profit.

What bad star could be enough to worry the Master of the Territory? It wasn't any of her concern, so she didn't ask, but the sense of not-understand, of knowing that she would never be able to understand, came back like a slap to the face, leaving her skin burning and her chest tight.

Like the man who'd been tied to the post, she wanted to hit something, to hurt something in return.

The devil paused halfway into the room, rolling down his sleeves as he looked around. Although there were thumps and low voices coming from upstairs where the others were now bathing or dressing for the day, it was still only the four of them in the front room. From the expression on the boss' face, he hadn't realized it was still so early. Or he didn't know why they were just sitting there, rather than making their hands busy.

"J udit told you last night to stay in bed," the boss told Antonia. He moved to the bar, and raised two fingers toward Iktan. The bartender retrieved a bottle from under the counter, the gentle clink of glass on wood louder than it should have been.

"Bored of bed," Antonia said, her tone gone sulky, making a face down at her mug, which had finally stopped steaming, then eying the remaining eggs as though they'd given offense.

"If you'd just—"

She looked up, narrowing red-rimmed eyes at him as though daring him to continue, and he held up one hand in mocking surrender. "Your choice."

"Thank you," she said, her tone now dripping with bitter honey, and he laughed, some of the tension sliding off his face. Then she sneezed again, and sighed. "I'll just get some more tea, and then I'll go back," she said, rising from her chair, and disappearing through the wooden slat doors into the kitchen.

And then it was just the boss, Iktan, and Grace.

Iktan poured a glass of something dark brown and set it by the boss' elbow. He picked it up, then turned to her, elbow leaning against the bartop as though he had all the hours in the day.

She thought she should make her excuses, go back upstairs, or into the kitchen to see if there were chores that needed doing, but instead she remained, caught as though something had nailed her shoes to the floor.

"You've something you wanted to ask me." It wasn't a question, as though he'd expected to find her waiting here, when he emerged. Perhaps he had. If he knew what strangers desired without them having to voice it, why should she be any less obvious to him, living under his roof.

Or maybe he simply couldn't conceive of any other reason she'd be dressed and waiting.

Did she have something to ask him? She did, she remembered, the discussion having nearly driven her earlier worries from her mind. If she had any sense, she would shake her head, laugh it off, make the best of what she had, as best she could.

But she was tired. Tired of *herself.* "What are you?"

"Interesting question," he said, taking a sip from his glass and nodding approval at Iktan. "Somewhat rude, but interesting."

She scoffed, watching him move from the bar to his table, drink in hand. "I would know who I work for. Only a fool would think you were human."

"And I brook no fools under my roof," he agreed. He reached for the first of three paper-wrapped decks on the table, and examined the seal on it. "Does it truly matter, what I am—or am not?"

She stepped forward, taking one of the seats across the felt from him. If she was going to challenge him, she should do it properly. "Everything matters. It's only a question of how much, and to whom."

"Truth," he acknowledged. "But what I am is not what digs at you, is it?"

Her fingertips were cold, and she tucked them into her palm to warm them. He saw far too much, with those whisky eyes. But she'd never been very good at subtlety, and saw no reason to humiliate herself further now, in trying.

"When I first came here, they told me people ride into Flood because they have business with you."

"Also truth."

"Some people, though, they come to see what you

are, because they're curious. Because you're the Master of the Territory, and hold their fates in your hands."

His hands never stilled, stripping the wax seal and shuffling the first deck into his free hand. "That is what some believe."

"I had no business with you. I wasn't curious. I didn't know you existed."

She had never thought to come here, would never have come here, on her own. But she had entered a crossroads at high noon, when the winds were strong and strange, and even if she'd known—even if she'd known, she still would have taken that turn.

Maybe she *was* mad.

The devil set down the opened pack, and picked up another.

"Some folk come to test themselves against you. To say that they did. Face the devil and walk away unscathed. But—" and she paused, searching for the correct words. "I feel no need to test myself. I am what I am, and you are ... whatever you are."

"And that doesn't bother you."

"No." She supposed it should. She had been raised a decent Christian, though she had never felt a particular call to worship, the way some did, and the devil...

He wasn't the devil, of course. Not truly.

But he made deals—and he kept them. If you wanted—needed—something badly enough.

"Everyone wants something from you. And you ... know what they want, what they need. How?"

How could he do it, how could he read people the way Judit read her cards?

The devil works in mysterious ways, they said. Or mayhap it was she who was lacking.

He laughed a little, almost under his breath. "Desire."

That was what Zinnia had said. She shook her head, still not understanding.

"Desire is human. It's blood and brain and spine all tangled up in the heart. Causes more trouble than it solves, but nothing would be solved without it." He slit open a new pack of cards and fanned them out on the felt, scanning the colored backs for any imperfection or crease. "Some think to use it to control others, but I've noted it's the one thing that makes folk uncontrollable. You, though. You're something else, and that's a fact."

She bit her lip hard enough to taste the flesh underneath. She wanted, she'd always *wanted*. And now he was telling her ... what? That she didn't want enough? That no matter how she tried, she wasn't good enough?

She's not natural. There's something just not right about her. Voices from the past, whispers when she should have been sleeping, beetles burrowing under her skin and setting up in her thoughts. Months of restlessness, chasing her even cross-River. The winds had been wrong: there was nothing for her here.

She stood, the chair pushing back behind her, and, unable to find the words to express what she felt, grabbed the nearest thing to-hand and threw it at him.

There was silence, which made the tiny pink-plink-plink of dripping yolk all the more obvious, as it gathered on his chest and fell with a splatter to the floor.

She felt something clawed dig into her chest, her spine stiffening in reaction, that violent urge to strike out replaced by horror that she had actually done so, and done so to the *boss*.

But layered over all that a bubbling sense of hysteria that she had done it, not with her knife, or her nails, or even her voice, but the *eggs*.

"I'd thought they were meant to be taken internally,

not externally," a voice said, and it took her an indrawn breath to realize that it was the boss. That he was running a finger through the mess and held the finger up for inspection.

"I ... I'm ..." There was no way to say she was sorry: they both knew she wasn't, and while she'd become accustomed to hiding her thoughts, lying about them was a sin she'd tried to avoid.

"She's as much a devil as you," Iktan said, and the boss ... laughed. And once started, it seemed almost as though he couldn't stop, a hand thumping against his chest with a hollow beat, the rich tone of his chuckles filling the silence entirely, until it was all she could hear.

She risked a sideways glance at Iktan. He was leaning on the bar, fingers folded together, the wrinkles on his face softly calm as he waited for the boss to compose himself again.

But that seemed to almost set the boss off again, until he reached for the chair he'd knocked over when she'd egged him, righting it and folding himself down into it, his free hand gesturing for her to do the same. She remained standing, instead.

His laughter, rather than amusing, made her angrier, mortification heating her cheeks. It wasn't enough, all of this, but he *laughed* at her?

"You're angry." The boss tilted his head at her, his expression puzzled, as though he couldn't imagine why he might be upset, why anything about any of this might anger her. As though she were the odd one, the out of place one.

Again.

She welcomed the fury that filled her then, the heat of it pushing out uncertainty and confusion.

People wanted things, Zinnia had said. Desire is human, the boss claimed. She'd only wanted one thing her entire life, but it hadn't ever done her any good, had it? Only odd looks and awkward breaks in conversation, only her father's pity and her mother's worry, sideways glances and whispered gossip.

She had never asked for special treatment, had never expected to have to do anything but pretend. She knew better than to think she—odd, unlovely, ungentle—could ever be anything other than the odd one, the difficult one. The one who couldn't quite be trusted, for reasons no-one would name. Not demure enough, not loving enough, not brilliant enough to be forgiven or explained away. An entire life spent on the fringe, rather than the weave.

She'd thought the Territory would be the place where she could fit, where she made sense, rather than forever having to reshape herself to fit others, constantly biting back words rather than speaking her mind. Had thought the devil himself would know what to do with her.

Why else would the winds have blown her there?

But the winds were uncanny, even in an uncanny place, and she had been warned not to think them helpful.

She'd done so anyway. Had *hoped*, even though she'd never let herself think it.

"Iktan." The boss didn't say anything more, but the bartender nodded once, and slipped from behind the bar and out the front door, closing it gently behind him. In the silence that followed, she heard the scratch and snick of a match, and the wet puffing noise of a cigar being lit.

The devil passed a hand over the front of his shirt, and the debris speckling the cloth disappeared. He then sat back in his chair and waited for her to do the same.

She stood her ground.

"Talk to me, Grace."

She had spent too many years holding back to let her thoughts loose now.

He studied her, looked at her, the way he had the first day she came. She stared back, then dropped her gaze to the floor.

"You're afraid." He sounded almost surprised, he who was never surprised by anything. "Of yourself. Oh, little one, of all the things to fear in this world, yourself should never be one of them."

"You said it true. I'm not like the others. I don't … feel things the way they do. I don't react properly. Even here."

Even her *thoughts* had disturbed Zinnia into sleeplessness.

"And do you think Zinnia was frightened? That was why she crept into your chamber, to speak you to rest, because she was frightened?"

She made an effort not to be frightening. But people still knew. Even when she tried to hide it. She didn't feel right. She *couldn't* feel right.

"Do you think that's why Bets tells you her dreams, her hopes? Or why Louis teaches you how to sharpen his beloved knives? Because you frighten them?"

She didn't understand why any of them did any of that. She didn't understand *them*. Had never understood their desire to bring her closer, or why they would be foolish enough to want that. All she had inside her was violence and anger, a spindle too-tightly wound, that would snap if she tried to use it.

She'd been born wrong. Her mother had known it, had warned her about it. "Pretend," she'd told her daughter. "Pretend, and everything will be all right."

She'd pretended, and thought it would be enough. But it wasn't, and she had nowhere else to try.

"You think your desire was not enough?" The boss shook his head, all humor gone from his eyes and mouth. "Oh, little one. You were aching with it, so hard I could feel you through the currents, like a shockwave when you hit the shore. The winds sensed you as easily as I did. But you weren't ready for us yet."

Her anger shifted, the uncertainty returning, making her shift on her feet, suddenly awkward and uncomfortable. "I don't understand."

"No, I don't suppose you do. That's the problem, not that you don't know, but you don't understand what you know."

She narrowed her eyes at him; he was doing that thing he did, that was only amusing when he did it to other people.

Her glare put the amusement back into his eyes, and he gestured to the chair opposite him again. "Would you care to play a game of cards, to discuss the matter?"

She eyed the pieces of board scattered on the felt, and shook her head. "I don't have enough to wager, and I'd rather not be further in debt to you."

He chuckled. "That makes you wiser already than most who ride in here. But I knew that already, too."

Her eyes narrowed ever further, until she could feel the lines forming at the edges of her eyes. "Can't you just tell me whatever it is you're planning on telling me?"

"I could, but where would be the fun in that?" His eyes went flat. "Sit down, Grace."

She pulled the chair out from the table, and sat down.

"If you didn't belong here, you wouldn't be here."

He said it so calmly, he might have been discussing the whiskey in his glass, but the words felt like a blow to her throat; to have him say it left no room for dissent, no room for doubt. And yet...

"The winds blew me here." A saying, back in the States. But the winds were a true thing, here. Dangerous, and true. The winds had sensed her, the boss said. But why had they taken an interest in her?

"The winds have their reasons and nothing mortal should try to understand them," the boss agreed, and she wondered if he could hear what she did not say, as well. "Not unless they are willing to pay the price. That takes nothing from the fact that even they knew: if you didn't belong here, you would not have come here."

She bit the inside of her lips, as though to force them to stay shut, and shook her head. If she belonged here, shouldn't she *feel* it?

"People cross the river for as many reasons as there are people. There isn't anyone who deserves to be here, or who should be here. Only people who choose to be here." His own lips quirked a little. "With the provision that we are discussing settlers; the I'i'yatchi, the born-here, they have their own stories and their own ways of learning who they are. Part of the Agreement is to allow those who might become I'i'yatchi to find their way."

Unwillingly, Grace found herself distracted. "That's a tribe?"

"It's a people," he said. "Less to do with where you're born and more about why you're born." He tilted his glass at her. "And that's a worry you needn't take on. Let me and Marie fret over that, when the time comes."

She shook her head again, unsure who Marie might be, but didn't interrupt to ask.

"You—" and he stopped, but didn't look away from her. His features were dark-shaded now, his hair a fine-spun thatch of moonlight, and for a breath, his eyes flickered with the silver of the moon.

She heard the sound of feet on the stair behind her, then they stopped halfway down and retreated. She didn't turn around to see who it had been.

"The thing most don't understand. The Territory isn't here for you. Not you, nor me, nor anyone. It simply is. It's ... a space. Nothing less—but also nothing more."

"A space you protect." The stories she had heard back home said the devil had claimed these lands, that to come here was to abandon all hope of salvation. Within these lands, they called him the Master of the Territory. But he acted the master of nothing, not even his saloon.

She didn't understand that, either.

A gentle shrug, the smell of black tobacco, brimstone, and whisky settling thick in the air. "I maintain a balance. The push and pull of conflicting needs. People come to me because they know what they need, but not how to find it."

I want to belong, she wanted to say, to yell, to howl. But the words stuck in her throat.

"When they are ready, they come to me. What they need, I arrange—for a price. Often a high price."

She scoffed a little at that. "I've never seen you take anything save coin in exchange. And you don't care about coin."

"Silver coin has its uses, and I welcome it to my pocket, but no. To gain desire, you must give something meaningful."

She had nothing to give. Not even coin, any more.

The devil leaned back in his chair, the cards slipping between his fingers in an effortless shuffle. "You will. When you're ready."

I t took her four more months to be able to speak what she needed, fingers clenched and head bowed before him, until he lifted her chin, golden eyes filled with understanding she barely understood herself.

And if the price he asked was high, it seemed little enough for what she received.

S ound carried in the Territory. Seven months on the road, and she was still not accustomed to how the call of birds, the scolding chirps of ground-mice, even the far-overhead cries of hawk and buzzard could seem as ear-close as her hat. Most, she had learned to ignore the way she ignored the weight of her hat pulled low on her forehead, the absence of them more a warning than their presence. Most, but not all.

She reined her mule in and listened again, the mule's cocked ear telling her it'd heard the sound, too. Something was out there, in the tall grass.

The first stretch of dawn had washed the stars away in a hot pink haze, promising another day of clear blue skies, the faint crackle of summer heat still only a hint of what was to come. She planned to be well out of the plains by then, although she had no clear thought of where. She was bound by nothing, now, save her own whim and nature.

She would not follow the winds, not in the manner of a magician, but often enough, they offered suggestion. Some might find that of concern; she had learned to accept it. They were uncanny; but so too was she.

The thought still made her smile, even as she

considered her surroundings. If an ambush were to come, it would likely come now. The high plains that had been her home for months had slowly given way to wind-struck foothills and worryingly-shaped pillars of rock, capable of hiding a multitude of threats, and she still had to contend with the tall grasses that made every road a risk, offering cover to whatever might prowl alongside.

She feared nothing, welcomed violence, but that did not make her incautious.

The molly's sides heaved, a sure sign that it was unhappy staying still, and she pressed her legs against its sides more firmly, reminding it who made the decisions. She preferred the mule to human company; it heeded her, without argument, unhappy but compliant.

Although the sound was not repeated, she still slipped the rib-knife from the sheath under her jacket. She had another at her thigh, and a longer one on the molly's saddle, but they would be useless on horseback. The rib-knife was better for throwing. The Territory was unforgiving of fools; best always be ready.

No sooner had the thought come than there was a burst of motion in the tall grass to her left. The knife flicked into her palm, her muscles tensing even as the molly shifted, still wanting to run but waiting for a signal.

A tussle of limbs and tails fell out of the grasses, nearly at the molly's hooves, and it did dance back then, ears twitching until she laid a firmer hand on the reins with one hand, the other still balancing the knife.

The limbs resolved themselves into a young man, dark haired and tawny-skinned, and a demon, ash-grey and scale-green, its tail whipping furiously enough she forgave herself for thinking there was more than one.

She studied the figures, noting that they seemed

evenly matched, and wondered if she was supposed to intervene. People did odd things for odd reasons....

But she was not people. She was herself, and she had no coin in this game. But neither could she ride on, until they were out of her way.

There was a flash of metal—a knife in the boy's hand, or maybe a demon's claw, and a spray of blood—red, human, she noted—splashed onto the dirt. They scuffled a few seconds longer, silent save for the grunts she had heard earlier, until the demon landed on top, claws reaching for the boy's face.

It might not kill the boy, but it would leave a nasty and permanent scar, if he survived.

At the last second, the boy turned sharply, knocking the demon off-balance enough that he could eel out of its grasp, wiggling to momentary safety a few feet away while they both tried to catch their breath. She chuckled, and—either because it heard her, or smelled her, the demon noted her presence. It turned its head slantways and bared its teeth at her—a threat or a warning, she couldn't be certain. The molly shifted uneasily, wanting to either run or kick, and she silently told it to stay, using her legs and weight to calm it down, then tilted her own head, waiting for the demon to decide its next action.

She did not fear the demon, nor the youth, though in other moments he might have taken her mule, her knives, mayhap even her life, if he thought it would earn him acclaim, and some coin. She would not have begrudged it of him, if he had succeeded. Nor would she begrudge the demon if it chose to attack, though she would assuredly kill it. That was their nature, its and hers.

The demon's snarl flickered into something she might have called uncertainty under her poised regard, flat nostrils flaring as though scenting the faint brimstone she'd been told still lingered on her, then its wide-set eyes narrowed, and it lurched—not at her, but the boy, who—ignoring her entirely—had used its brief distraction to rise into a crouch. They collided with a meaty thunk, grappling for control, and disappeared into the grasses on the other side of the road, the tall stalks quivering in their passing until the grunting and rustling faded back to silence.

Her mouth twitched slightly, the ghost of laughter in her ears. No-one knew what demon got from these encounters, if they had some ritual purpose, or simply to amuse themselves in the endless roll of days, or if there was no intent, only reaction. But if the boy survived, he would go home with enough of a story to earn himself a new name.

She wondered if the white woman and the spotted mule would play a role, if she would be an earth-spirit, another demon, or overlooked entirely in the retelling.

Perhaps he would assign her a new name, to replace the one she had Bargained away. If so, she would never know, would never be called by it. Never called to heel by it.

Names claimed, identified. Bound and obligated. Names had power.

All that was behind her, now.

The devil had taken her name, and set her free to follow the west winds.

She pushed her hat back, and looked up at the sky. Overhead, only two pairs of dark wings curved in widening circles, looking for prey, or something already dead to feast upon. Larger than the earlier hawks, but too small to be Reapers. She was almost disappointed; she'd heard stories of the beasts, but never seen one.

Not yet, anyhow. It had only been seven months

since she rode out of Flood, nameless and free, and there was much still to discover. A lifetime of discovery.

The mule's ears flicked forward, then back as though to say "well? Are we going to go, or not?"

"Cha, go then," she said, and they went on.

And enjoy a preview of Gabriel's Road,
coming in Winter 2019!

I t took the man too long to build a fire, his hands
stiff and chilled, his mind waterlogged and
reluctant. The flint seemed equally reluctant to
catch, the kindling branches he had gathered reluctant
to burn, as though the printed skin of his fingertips
made them damp as well, despite their crackling
dryness. He was rain and river, creek and spring, and
fire fled from him as though he might douse it.

He looked down at his hands, half-expecting them to
flow like water, blue-clear and liquid, rather than bone
and flesh. But he saw only skin under the bright
moonlight, tanned and rough, the nails smooth, the beds
below them clean and pink.

He flexed the fingers holding the flint, noting the
way the way the knucklebones shifted. There was
something about bones he was supposed to remember
…

Behind him, something moved, and he stilled, before
something still in memory recognized it as not-a-threat,
familiar, belonging.

Horse. The warm shape moving behind him was a

horse. His mind's eye described the gelding without having to look back, square head and low haunch, along with the knowing that the horse was his, and that it would alert him if danger came from behind.

He was not alone. That thought focused his hands enough to strike tinder properly, a tiny red spark dropping onto the kindling, and he moved without conscious thought, cradling the infant flame until it spread, placing larger pieces of kindling in a pattern until they caught in return, then carefully placing small branches around it, gauging the proper moment to place more over the flame, until the fire leapt up, embracing the fuel, and settling itself into a steady blaze.

He held his hands out to the flame, letting warmth slowly return. How long had he been cold? Not long, not because the cold felt like a new thing, but rather because he had not been aware of being cold, before. Before what, he was not certain, and he shied away from that gap. But damp, the damp he had been aware of, and that awareness made him shiver in revulsion, although he could not entirely remember why, only that the need to be dry, bone to skin, suddenly rode him.

But when he went to remove his clothing, thinking the cloth must be sodden, he discovered that no moisture lingered, that even his fingers, water-pruned though they looked, had no drops clinging to them.

But he had been damp. Had been soaked, drenched, as though he'd been submerged—

Let it come and let it go a voice said, and he thought for a crazed instant it had been the horse, before recognizing it as a memory. A memory of—

Old Woman Who Never Dies.

And as though the medicine woman had placed her hands on him once again, he remembered.

His horse, Steady, was behind him, and the fire was

before him, and his name was Gabriel, Gabriel Kasun, also known as Two Voices.

And he had left Isobel in Red Stick.

H e should have been by her side, at her back, ready to lend whatever support she needed. Instead, he had ridden out to face the Mudwater. Had ridden to the edge of the river, and ...

And done what?

The gap remained there, red-hazed and terrifying, and he stepped back from it, not yet ready to look deeper.

He had left Isobel. That thought returned to him, laden with the iron weight of guilt. Never mind that she was well-equipped to deal with the situation, that she was the only one who *was* equipped to deal with it, never mind that he knew he had taught her and taken her as far as he could. Never mind that he had not left her alone, that the marshal was with her, that ...

He had left her without a word, without a warning, driven by his own weakness and fear, and he had no sense of how long ago that had been, or where he was, now.

That thought, finally, made him look around.

He was in a shallow meadow, a hill rising directly to his left, the grass silvered under the full moon and starlight, a ridge of trees standing showed sentinel halfway up, while to his right and front, the meadow sloped gently before rising again. And behind him ....

He took a deep breath before turning to look.

The wide, flat ribbon of the Mudwater lay behind him, glimmering distant enough that he thought there must be two, three day's steady ride between them, and no road to tell him how he had gotten there, although, when he reached down, he could feel the steady thrum of the Road somewhere nearby. He might have ridden madcap across the valley, or found some trail, or—

His thoughts swerved away from how he had gotten there to what he had left behind. Isobel. *Izzy.* She had been his responsibility, and he had abandoned her.

The guilt dug its iron weight claws into his chest, but with it also a sense of sick relief. He did not know how long it had been since he left Red Stick, but he knew that it had been long enough that there was no going back. Whatever had happened was long done, and if she had succeeded or failed, it was her story now, not his.

The devil could do what he would with him, if he felt the Bargain had not been upheld. Gabriel could not find the strength in him to object.

And the Devil's Hand?

Something made the corner of his lip tick up, in what almost might have been a smile. She would rail at him, no doubt, when they encountered each other again. But he thought mayhap she would forgive him. Eventually.

If she survived.

That made the smile disappear, and he pressed a clenched fist against his chest, hard enough the bone underneath ached.

She lived. He knew it, once he thought to ask, rock-solid and certain as he knew the Road beneath him and the moon overhead.

"Thank you," he whispered to whatever had brought him that news, and let his hand fall back down to his lap.

Memories filtered back to him, slowly, and he knew they were not yet complete. But he had done his duty by Isobel. His Bargain with the devil was done.

You would be in my debt, if you did this, the devil had said. But there was no debt when you made Bargain with the devil, only payment. And while Gabriel had ridden into the town of Flood thinking to test himself against the Master of the Territory, facing him across the green felt of his own card table, in the end he had not wanted anything the devil had to offer.

And his offer to mentor the young girl he'd met in that salon, she of the strong-boned face and fine eyes, should she choose the way of the Road? That offer had been made not to the devil but Isobel herself; that the Old Man had accepted on her behalf should not change that. Gabriel had assumed that any payment the devil might intend would be made only when—if—Gabriel returned to Flood with her, presented her mentorship ride as completed.

But if the devil never lied, he was neither obligated to tell all the truth. And Gabriel had begun to suspect, far too late, that payment would be made far before return, far before he was ready—or willing—to accept.

They had ridden into Red Stick because that was where Isobel needed to be. But the moment he had come within sight of the Mudwater, Gabriel had been ill at ease, restless in bone and blood, and if he had told himself at first it was due to the unease within the Territory itself, the dis-ease Isobel Devil's Hand had been called to purge, he had known, at the end, that it was more.

He had been born with water-sense—dowsing, they called it elsewhere. He could feel the flow of fresh water, be it deep under his feet or running the surface of the earth. And he had resented it, not for the advantage it gave him, but the hold it claimed on him, the way it tied him to the Territory when his ambitions had fared elsewhere. Those the Territory claimed with its gifts, it did not easily let go.

He had come back when it called him, when it

cursed him with blood-sick. But he had never forgiven it, for all that he had relearned to love it. For all that he was able to show Isobel how to survive within it.

And if he were wracked by that unease, he was useless to Isobel. Worthless to himself. And so he had gone to the river's edge, and....

The water had lapped at his toes, brackish-brown, not the red of his walking-dreams, the familiar stink of rotting logs settling at the base of his nostrils, and he had felt it reach out and up, an unrelenting roll that would take and drown him, if he let it.

Old Woman had told him to let it come, and let it go. Instead, he had buried himself deep under resignation and inevitability, under the knowledge that the Territory was stronger than he, would always be strong; that the only resistance he could make would be to refuse to let it own him entirely. And that kernel he kept, it was his alone. So long as he held onto it, he could remain his own man.

But the Territory itself was under siege, from enemies without, and dissension within. The Agreement teetered on the frail strength of human will, and he could do nothing more than stand by and let Isobel—barely grown, barely done with her mentorship ride—shoulder that weight alone.

He could not see the Devil's Hand, in that moment, only the girl-child he had willingly, willfully taken responsibility for.

He would have failed. Again.

"Have done with me," he had told the power that was the River, not shouting in anger nor crying in fear, but calmly, in the voice of a man who had gone as far as he could, until the rope of his mortality caught him and he could strain no more. "Have done with me, once and for all, either let me go or finally drown me, once and for all."

And the River had ....

The sensation of damp chill settled within him once again. He could not recall anything beyond that moment, save that the River had called him, and—for once, against his will—he had gone.

"What have you done to me," he whispered, and thought he heard the devil's laughter, not cruel or mocking, but amused at the thought that a mortal could avoid payment, once their Bargain was done.

He forced himself to breathe, once and then twice, inhaling deeply and then exhaling slowly, until the fluttering panic subsided, and he was back firmly within his own flesh again. The fire crackled warm at his front, the air was night-cool and still on his skin, and he felt neither hunger not exhaustion, despite having no memory of the past few days of eating or sleeping, or anything at all.

He had thought—had believed—that if he did not return to claim his reward from the devil, it would not be awarded. He wondered, now, what sort of fool he had been, to think it would be that simple.

And yet ...

He wiggled his toes within his boots, shook out his shoulders, straightened his spine and then let it curve forward again, reaching inward for the sense that had always dogged him, the water-sense that had driven him for as long as he could remember, and likely the times he could not remember, as well.

Nothing had changed. It was still contained, still controlled. Whatever had happened when he confronted the Mudwater, whatever had crept within him, nothing of *him* had changed.

That was a relief, and yet.

And yet nothing in his life let him believe it was that simple.

Suddenly, he wanted nothing more than to swing into the saddle, to ride as far and as fast as he could, to leave the Mudwater so far behind no-one he spoke to had ever seen it.

Even as he thought that, Gabriel mocked himself. He had tried that once, crossing it and heading east, into the States, to lose himself in the teeming cities, keeping his back to the indifferent Atlantic, his mind on the foibles of human Law and nature. And he had suffered for it, becoming so ill he'd no choice but to return.

"I belong to nothing and no-one save myself."

A memory surfaced, spreading circles around it. He had told Grandmother River that, and Grandmother River had …

His mind shied away, as though a rattlesnake had lifted its tail in warning, and his stomach tilted and churned in upset.

Something had happened, when he'd gone to confront the Mudwater, and he knew he should remember, knew that it was important that he remember. And that was the very last thing he wanted to do.

About the Author

Laura Anne Gilman's work has been hailed as "a true American myth being found" by NPR, praised for her "deft plotting and first-class characters" by Publishers Weekly, and has been shortlisted for the Nebula Award, the Endeavor Award, and the Washington State Book Awards. Her novels include the Locus-bestselling weird western series, (*Silver On The Road, The Cold Eye,* and *Red Waters Rising*), the long-running Cosa Nostradamus urban fantasy series, and the "Vineart War" trilogy, as well as the short story collection *Darkly Human*. Her short fiction has recently appeared in *Daily Science Fiction, Lightspeed,* and *The Underwater Ballroom Society*.

A former New Yorker, she currently lives outside of Seattle with two cats and many deadlines. More information, social media links, and updates can be found at www.lauraannegilman.net.

Also by Laura Anne Gilman

The Devil's West
Silver on the Road
The Cold Eye
Red Waters Rising

Other works available via Book View Cafe
From Whence You Came: A Lands Vin Novella

Darkly Human: 18 Stories
Dragon Virus

Sylvan Investigations
Miles to Go
Promises to Keep
The Work of Hunters
An Interrupted Cry

About Book View Café

Book View Café Publishing Cooperative (BVC) is an author-owned cooperative of over fifty professional writers, publishing in a variety of genres such as fantasy, romance, mystery, and science fiction.

BVC authors include New York Times and USA Today bestsellers; Nebula, Hugo, and Philip K. Dick Award winners; World Fantasy Award, Campbell Award, and RITA Award nominees; and winners and nominees of many other publishing awards.

Since its debut in 2008, BVC has gained a reputation for producing high-quality ebooks, and is now bringing that same quality to its print editions.

CPSIA information can be obtained
at www.ICGtesting.com
Printed in the USA
LVHW041547230822
726649LV00004B/175

9 781611 387728